George W. Steevens

Egypt in 1898

George W. Steevens

Egypt in 1898

ISBN/EAN: 9783337230494

Printed in Europe, USA, Canada, Australia, Japan

Cover: Foto ©Andreas Hilbeck / pixelio.de

More available books at **www.hansebooks.com**

EGYPT IN 1898

BY

G. W. STEEVENS

AUTHOR OF

" The Land of the Dollar,"
" With the Conquering Turk."

NEW YORK
DODD, MEAD & COMPANY
1899

CONTENTS.

I.

THE IMPERIAL HIGHWAY.

II.

PORT SAID.

III.

IN SEARCH OF THE EAST.

IX.

AN EGYPTIAN ETON.

X.

A DAY IN THE DESERT.

XI.

A NIGHT IN THE DESERT.

XII.

A COPTIC MONASTERY.

XIII.

TAMING THE DESERT.

XIV.

THE SUDAN AND THE FELLAH.

XV.

ALEXANDRIA.

XVI.

LORD CROMER AND HIS WORK.

XVII.

BITS OF OLD AND NEW.

XVIII.

THE PILGRIMS.

XIX.

THE PANORAMA.

XX.

THE RUINS.

XXI.

THE DAHABEAH.

XXII.

THE ANCIENT EGYPTIANS.

XXIII.

THROUGH NUBIA.

XXIV.

COOK.

XXV.

LOOKING BACK AND FORWARD.

ILLUSTRATIONS.

EGYPT IN 1898.

I.

THE IMPERIAL HIGHWAY.

THE PENINSULAR AND ORIENTAL EXPRESS — BRITISH EMPIRE-
BUILDERS — THE IMPERIAL ENGLISHMAN — BRINDISI — THE
MAIL-BAGS — A P. AND O. LINER — LASCARS — THE GATE OF
THE EAST.

December 11.—Sun? Not much sun here.
All day we had been ploughing hoarsely
through the monotonous prairie called France.
Now at dusk the Peninsular and Oriental
Express stood clammily at the little Alpine
station of St Jean - de - Something, a few
minutes from the frontier. The huge cube of
mountain above, with its sparse firs showing
on the table atop, like people on the Monu-

A

ment, was streaked and dappled with snow.
On either side of the track the snow was
piled a foot deep. As the two upstanding
mountain - engines panted and snorted, im-
patient to get to the top of the Mont Cenis
and down into the plain again, half-melting,
half-caking snow dribbled down every window. And I a seeker after sun! Ugh!

Rather stay and be frozen in one's own
country. Yet there are compensations everywhere, and even the P. and O. Express chill-
ing among the Alps offered an experience
with its own peculiar flavour. There was
nothing externally in the three long sleeping
and dining cars and three luggage-vans to
mark it off from any of the other "Grand
European Expresses" purveyed by the Sleep-
ing-Car Company. The beds were the same
—less comfortable than the American model,
because on the American plan you have a
broad bed, and can undress at ease in the
central gangway after the ladies have gone
to bed, instead of being boxed up in a four-
berth coop with luggage rising up from the

floor till it threatens to submerge the whole. The food was the same—and when I say that it was the Wagons-Lits food, I say all. It is a class of nourishment wholly by itself, whether you come on it in France, or Hungary, or darkest Turkey. Some like it and some don't. I don't.

The brown-uniformed attentive attendants were the same as everywhere — except, it suddenly struck you, that they all talked English. They all talked English—and there you got the clue to the peculiar character of the train. It was altogether an English train. So far it had not embarked a single passenger who was not a Briton. And their trade it was not difficult to see. Fair-haired and blue-eyed, square-shouldered and square-jawed, with puckered brows and steadfast eyes that seemed to look outwards and inwards at the same time, self-contained, self-controlled, and self-reliant, they were unmistakably builders —British empire-builders. The faces of the women were serene with the imperturbable serenity of those who have seen too many

strange sights to be surprised now at anything; and in their patient aspect was a hint
of the tragic heroism that sends its children
to be brought up by strangers and forget
their mothers.

The Empire-builders were going forth to
their long work again. This man was going
to his collectorship in the Central Provinces,
that to his tea-plantation in Assam. This
grey-haired merchant was for Brisbane; that
pale-faced lady had brought home her children, and was hurrying back to her husband
in Hong-Kong. The ruddy subaltern was
only going out to have a shot for the Gippy
army; but the jolly little man in a wig beside
him would not be done till some snail of a
local steamer, after many changes, dumped
him down under a verandah in Manila. To
every point of the remotest East were return-
ing, quite uncomplaining, the obscure makers
of the British empire. It was a geography
lesson in itself—and remember that this train
leaves London every Friday night, and that
its freight is always the same. Thinking this,

you saw that the two engines, three cars, and three vans were no ordinary train after all. They were a very vital link in that band of scarlet that grips the world—the British empire. Thinking of the load of heavy hearts it bore, of self-sacrifice, of single-eyed, unquestioning duty-doing, you began for the hundredth time to say that you never before had quite realised what "British empire" means.

December 12.—Sun! I felt it in the close-curtained berth before ever I opened my eyes. When I did open them, a foot below the car-roof, little yellow beams were stabbing through every chink. When I leapt down and got out into the corridor, we were ripping smoothly down the eastern side of Italy. The sky was blue—not that pale irresolute bluish, but blue—blue all over, from horizon to horizon, with a straightforward, thick, solid blue, as if it liked it. And bathing the pale grass, shimmering with silver on the olive-trees, burnishing the far line of the white-capped Apennines, steeping the wooden sides of the train and the

starved temperaments of its passengers, was
the blessed sun. On our left was the Adriatic,
and all day, as the sun warmed it, it grew
bluer and bluer. The sun was not hot, and
the leafless trees and brown fallows forbade
the delusion that it was summer. Yet it was
honest, uncompromising sunshine all the same,
and if it did not warm the body very much, it
thawed the spirit. The sun of the south is a
sensation of itself. As soon as it shines on
you, you begin to feel that the things which
brought care before do not perhaps matter so
very much after all. You begin insensibly to
alter your standards of the importance of all
things. Time, for instance, doesn't matter;
trouble does. It suddenly strikes you what
a heavy, clumsy device is a tobacco-pipe, which
needs to be carried about in a pocket, and not
merely lit but filled. How much simpler and
lighter to smoke a cigarette! That change in
your British strenuousness symbolises much.

To the Imperial Englishmen in the train,
also, the sun was welcome; it has become a
second climate. Not that it dispels care for

them. But no sun or storm can shake the steady independence of the British character when you get it at its best. This was to be seen in little things during the long day's run down Italy. When you see men of other nations on the third day of a railway journey, they are generally unkempt to look at and unwholesome to sit by. The precise, imperturbable, Imperial Englishman takes off all his clothes, and goes to bed cleanly in his pyjamas; he bathes standing up, and shaves religiously each morning, and carefully brushes his clothes. He talks little, although there is a freemasonry about the smoking-room of the P. and O. Express which melts down great part of his native reserve. When he does talk, it is not of money, like the travelling American, nor of beer and time-tables, like the travelling German, but of sport. The foreigner in like case makes talking his main business; the Englishman appears to throw out his talk as a kind of afterthought and accompaniment to smoking. On to the cloud of tobacco smoke floats occasionally a brief reminiscence of many woodcock, or a hint to the young pig-sticker. It is not exactly conversation, and it is not at all wittily put; but all the same, if you do happen to be interested about such things, you perceive that the man who says a thing usually knows what he is talking about.

As the sun slanted down we were obviously drawing near Brindisi; the whole population of the Express with one accord began to write home. The letters did not appear to run very fluently, and were probably not masterpieces of literature. But they were letters home, which means a deal more to the Englishman than Shakespeare and Milton will ever do— the first letters home, the first, it was pathetic to think, of how many! It was pathetic to wonder how many of these taciturn, decidedly uninspired, all but commonplace men had made themselves widowers and childless in the interests of the British empire. You might wonder; but of course they didn't say anything about it. It was their business, and they were doing it. Duty has got to be done in the proper place, at the proper time, in spite of all things. Just as at the proper time and in spite of all things—a standing rebuke to the kingdom of Italy, where it alone is certain and punctual—the Imperial Express clanked into Brindisi.

December 13.—Two thousand five hundred mail-bags! So they said; at any rate there were twenty-seven railway vans of them, and it took nearly five hours last night and this morning to get them on board. As I sat in the smoking-room about ten, wondering when they were going to start, I heard a clatter and bumping outside, and went to look. Below the tall liner lay the broad quay and the white Italian houses of Brindisi; the yellow in their windows looked vulgar but cheerful beside the blue moonlight that bathed everything else. And up an enormous long gangway came the mails.

An endless string of Lascars brought them. Shuffling spectres climbing the gangway; then the sudden gleam of teeth in the moonlight; then, one by one, appeared a

solid bag and a solid pair of brown human
legs within the circle of electric lamps,
where sat the officers checking each bag.
Under the bag appeared a greasy red cloth;
under the cloth a brown grinning face, with
its features all cramped together in the
middle. An English sailor seized each Lascar
as he came up, and twisted him round till his
bag's name was under the light. "Sydney,"
cried the one officer. "Sydney; right,"
answered the other from the table. Then
the chief man of the Lascars, standing by—
magnificent in voluminous red turban, portly
blue smock, fat cheeks, and whiskers—seized
his subordinate, and pushed him forward in
the way he should go: the little wisp of
brown ugliness pattered off, faded again to
a spectre, was lost in the darkness of the
ship.

Then the next and the next; another
and another and another. Sydney, Bombay,
Hong - Kong, Queensland *via* Melbourne,
Queensland *via* Torres Straits, Aden, New
Zealand, Manila, Beyrout, King George's

Sound, Penang, and Launceston. Bags on bags of Christmas cards and New Year's greetings for England in the East; bags on bags of business and affection for the new Britain on the other side of the world. On and on they came endlessly—more ghosts up the gangway, more teeth gleaming devilishly out of demon faces, more dirty legs staggering into the lamplight under more mail-bags. Some were passed off one way, some another, till you would have said the ship would split asunder and bleed mail-bags all over the Adriatic. And still up, up they came. Are we not on the main highway of the British empire?

December 14.—I had always imagined a liner of the P. and O. as something peculiarly stately and luxurious—the lawful heir of the old East Indiaman. There is something in the very name "Peninsular and Oriental" that fills the ear and imagination. I was a trifle disappointed at first to find the Britannia only a ship after all. I did not expect her to be fast; P. and O. steamers

are not fast, and somehow one feels that it
would be flippancy to ask them to be. In
war-time, one feels sure, the cruising enemy
will remember that the P. and O. is the
oldest line east of Suez, and draw aside and
dip his ensign as the subsidised slug crawls
by. But it was rather painful to find the
smoking - room about half the size of an
Atlantic liner's, and decorated with green
tiles that recalled bedroom suites in Totten-
ham Court Road. The table, again, was not
what the letters P. and O. had seemed to
promise. That, at least, is the way I put
it : older travellers gloomily said it was just
what they expected. I have eaten far better on
dirty little tubs of the Messageries Maritimes
and Florio-Rubattino. Brawn is a very difficult viand to get really bad ; but such musty
brawn as exists on the world's markets seemed
to have been cornered by the cook of the
Britannia.[1]

---

[1] Since this was written, I am told, the P. and O. has sent
an inspector to inspect its food. So that possibly the brawn is
better now, and these criticisms out of date.

Yet the P. and O. grows on you; even in two days it grows on you. There is something stately about it, after all; and it is very English, to boot, and very picturesque. The ship is not a ferry-boat, like an Atlantic liner, but something between a hotel and a home. It is even more miraculously clean than other ships. The officers are point device in their smartness and courtesy; the very stewards have something of the grand manner of good servants. You dress decorously for dinner, and your cabin gives you plenty of room to dress in. You begin to realise that you are going to a part of the world where your people are sahibs, to be treated as such, and to behave as such; and then you see it would be hardly fitting for the P. and O. to scurry along at twenty-two knots an hour.

Then there is the family aspect of the ship, which conveys an impression of stability. There are babies with nurses—not in themselves objects of delight, but interesting because of the wonderful destiny that makes them at home half round the world before they know right hand from left. When the mothers bring the babies up on to the promenade-deck you get an illustration of the continuity of the British empire,—continuity in space, and continuity in time. These toddling nuisances are quite at home at sea. With many it is not their first voyage, nor their second. They are quite at home; their home from birth up is the world, wherever there may be work to do. Many of them, you know, will go on living till they die on ships and in queer torrid corners of the world. They will die earlier than we stay-at-homes, as their fathers and mothers, grandfathers and grandmothers, will have died before them. But they will not die, we hope, till they have got other infants to make themselves a nuisance about promenade-decks; and, die soon or late, it is odds on their having done a decent bit of work for their country and themselves.

The Lascars are another text for a little sermon on the importance of being English.

They are not beautiful, and they are not what you were brought up to consider able-bodied seamen. They appear to need almost as many white men to tell them what to do, and to push them into the proper positions to do it, as would more easily get through the work themselves. Every afternoon they do boat-drill : that is to say, a white quartermaster and their own leader put ten of them into position in a boat, and two are ready to lower away aft. It still wants two to lower forward, so the head Lascar goes off to find them. He is so long away that the quartermaster goes off to find him; then the Lascar comes back with his two; and presently the quartermaster comes with other two, and two are sent away, and two are fallen in with the four, and instantly dismissed again, and thank goodness that's over, and that's the sort of sailors Lascars are. People say their great merit is that they are quiet, and give no trouble; and they are fit enough, after all, to sweep decks and stretch out awnings. They never looked quite so picturesque again after that first night, as they brought in the mail - bags. But they finish off the picture of the empire-builders and the Imperial highway. They are a specimen of the raw material. Their very ugliness and stupidity furnish just the point. It is because there are people like this in the world that there is an Imperial Britain. This sort of creature has to be ruled, so we rule him, for his good and our own.

December 15.—To-day, for the first time, we woke up rolling out of sight of land. The day before yesterday it was the brown slopes of the Ionian Islands, with the snowy backbone of Greece behind them. Yesterday it was Crete — steeper brown slopes again tipped with a range of snow; and seeing Crete one long tangle of impossible mountains from west to east, you began to come to some comprehension of the immortality of the Cretan question. But alike yesterday and the day before and to-day we have run all day under an arch of blue. Each day

the blue has grown richer and more solid.
Each day the sun has shed himself upon us
more lavishly. We have let him soak in
and in, till to-day English winter is already
cleansed from the system. For, by now,
we are well in the south of the Levant; we
are already within touch of Egypt. The
day's run left twenty - three knots more to
go; at noon, and by lunch - time, we could
hardly be more than eight or nine away—
and yet no sign of it. Three-quarters of an
hour for lunch, and we must be tumbling
over it—yet still no sign. But, yes; there
on the starboard bow! There is a group of
dust - coloured houses, with a light tower,
quite close, not a mile away.

Only it seems to be standing on nothing,
in the middle of the sea. To port and starboard is still blue sea—nothing else at all.
We are getting much closer now, and we
see two low dust-coloured breakwaters pushing their snouts through the same blue sea.
Then some shipping near the houses — only
still no coast - line. The houses are Port

Said; the breakwaters are the Suez Canal;
and the land which you cannot see is ancient
Egypt, the cradle of human life. You seem
to have arrived at nowhere. None the less,
along the Imperial highway, we have now
come to the gate of the East.

Boats racing to a ship.

II.

PORT SAID.

December 16.—As we brought up at Port Said I cast a casual glance to starboard, and saw that we were attached by cables to what looked like a black island in mid-Canal. I took no heed of it; but, looking that way a moment later, saw it had drawn nearer. It seemed a great black raft, slowly warping itself nearer and nearer, and on it—what was moving?—by the Powers, they were men!

Men they were, and the raft was an enormous coal-lighter; only which was coal and which was lighter and which were men was more than anybody could say. So black a crew it carried, swarming like flies on a treacle-jar, on every inch of foothold to the water's edge. They seemed to wear shirt and drawers and a rag round the head; but, again, which was clothes and which was man? Clothes and skin were both grimed the same black with coal-dust. As they approached they set up a kind of wailing chant, and the white teeth flashing out were the only part of all the raft that was not coal-black. Once more I was looking at a crew of devils going through some unholy ritual of their devilry. Only the devilish-looking Lascars at Brindisi had been working in half-light and shadow; on these the high sun shone drily; everything round was refulgent, except that one murky blot on the water. Slowly and slowly, but nearer and nearer, howling and grinning, naked and black—till you thought the Canal must have opened and let up the sooty monster straight out of the Pit.

As the thing drew to the ship's side they heaved up four huge planks, two forward and two aft of the lighter, to the level of the high main-deck. And the moment they were in position — before, you would have said, the tottering bridges could possibly be stable— the devils had paused in their incantations, and got to work. Up the dizzy plank they came, tottering under rush-baskets piled up with coal. The slope was half perpendicular, and the planks were narrow, and some of the demons carried one basket on the head, and another in the arms. But they never slipped : their naked feet gripping the wood, one after another pattered up and plunged into the bowels of the ship. They still kept up their rising, falling lullaby, as one, two, three, half-a-dozen sprang on board, and hurried his freight into the bunkers. In a minute there was a complete chain of them, two rows tripping up with full baskets, two rows tripping down with empties. In the body of the lighter another gang of demons was hacking, and delving, and shovelling. More baskets leaping up full, more bounding down empty, more tilting, more lilting, more dust. This dust rose up round them in a choking cloud. And as I went ashore the last of it was a rolling pillar of blackness against the ship's side, and, dimly seen through it, a racing chain of devils up and down, with a forlorn and melancholy croon, working out the tale of their damnation.

December 17.—That melodramatic sight, I learn, is Port Said. That is just the essence and root of being of Port Said. Port Said is coal—the Clapham Junction of nations, the gate of East and West, the coaling-station of the world. Its native population is all made of coal-porters, and those that minister to them; its Europeans are in coal companies or connected with ships that need coaling. A million tons a-year is the figure of Port Said's coal-bill. It nearly all comes from Wales, and what does not comes from Newcastle; but in the main ships will burn nothing but Ocean Merthyr. Residents in Port Said expatiate on the beauties of Ocean Merthyr for domestic purposes also; but though I am quite ready to take their expert opinion about sun, I stick to my own about winter firing. "I wish I could show you a fire of it now," said one to me; "but we haven't a fire going to-day:" now what can a man who has no fire on December 17 know about house coals?

The ships' coal lies stored for the most part in the lighters, whence it is to be put aboard the vessels; it would not pay for landing One firm alone, the Port Said and Suez Coal Company, has lighter accommodation for 7000 tons at a time. And how astoundingly well the porter-demons can do their work is shown by the records of the same company for coaling the P. and O. Caledonia. On December 11, 1894, they put on board 602 tons in 70 min.; on January 21, 1895, 628 tons in 75 min.; on March 31, 812 tons in 100 min.; on December 22, 915 tons in 110 min. This is all comfortably over eight tons a minute —and the labourers do it on just a trifle over nothing a-day!

That, as I say, is Port Said—and there is nothing else. It is no wonder you do not see the land as you approach it; there is no land to see. The town lies on a little triangle of sand between the Canal and the salt swamps that fringe the Delta of the Nile. Until the Canal was cut, there was nothing there but birds' nests. Now there is a town of 35,000 souls—10,000 of them Europeans, if you include Greeks, and 5000 of these respectable, if you do not press the word too far. The people are of every race and tongue known, for Port Said is Levantine of the Levantines.

From my window it looks a Levantine paradise. I can see down a row of well-built, cool - plastered, three - storeyed houses, with white and French-grey window-shutters, clean-painted iron verandahs, and balconies on each storey. Below a thick carpet of acacias, starred with yellow pods as big as a big broad bean, hides the street. Even in the Arab quarter the houses are all of them fairly new and most of them tolerably clean; they are not humped together as in older Eastern towns. A town, you see from Port Said, can be Levantine and yet clean and airy; the streets, moreover, are well kept,

level, and broad, and there are quaint little
foot-gauge, one-mule tramways. Altogether,
you would say, a well-built, well-ordered,
well-liking little town.

But Port Said is not at all happy. It
owes its all to the Canal, but it has a notion
that the Canal owes it more yet. Besides
the coal, and the transhipment, and a little
provisioning, Port Said has no trade at all.
A twentieth part of its coal goes away to
Damietta, mostly as dust-and-clay briquettes
for cotton-mills; but what is that? Port
Said feels that it ought to be the great port
of Egypt. And so it ought, surely; for where
the ships are, there, on paper, ought the trade
to be. The million tons a-year has to go
away empty from Port Said, to Alexandria or
the Black Sea or anywhere it can, to get a
cargo to carry home again. If only the
Government would allow a proper railway
connection with Cairo and the interior, Port
Said would be the port of Egypt at once, as
Alexandria is and Damietta was. "Buy land
in Port Said," said an ancient resident; "and

you will be a rich man at sixty." It may be
so, though for myself I am not rich enough at
present to set the process going. But in any
case the Government hesitates to ruin Alexandria; so there is only a sort of steam-
tramway as far as Ismailia, where it joins
the Suez-Cairo Railway.

Another queer grievance of Port Said's own
is the electric light. You would not have
thought that the electric light would fill a
whole town with lamentation; but it has.
For some ten years it has enabled ships to
go through the Canal by night. Before that
every passing vessel had to lie the night at
Port Said, and those were the days — or
nights —of *café* concert, and roulette-table,
and dancing-saloon, bands crashing from dusk
to dawn, and gold flowing in torrents into the
lap of Port Said. In those nights a second-
engineer could start out with sixpence in his
pocket, and come back at sunrise with five
hundred pounds in his pocket and a knife in
his side. Now all that is gone. The shop-
keepers and pimps have only a brief sunshine

to get their hay in while the demons coal
ship; and the faster the demons coal, the
faster the money is aboard again and hull-
down out of sight of Port Said.

So Port Said is waiting—one eye regretfully on the golden, riotous past, one eye
dubiously on the golden industrious future.
It would be wonderful if it were not unhappy.
It is on the road to everywhere, and yet it is
on the road to nowhere. Ships pass every
day for every sea and port in the world—
except Port Said. On its Asiatic side is the
raw Arabian Desert. If you start to take a
walk on the African side you bring up against
a sopping shoal—a little salt water and then
a little sand, a basin of water and then a
bar of sand, sand and water, water and sand,
stretching dismally flat as far as you can see.
There are a few trees in the town, but hardly
a garden, and never a rood of green field; they
turn out their beasts on the beach. There are
no sights, no amusements, no society; everybody is saving his money for a summer somewhere else. Individuals are waiting as well

as the town—waiting to be sent somewhere
else. So they preserve their packing-cases
carefully marked with the household effects
that go inside them, and purvey coal.

December 18.—One moment, you will say.
I am leaving out the one great distinction of
Port Said, am I not? You expected a few
telling particulars about its abysmal vice.
Well, its abysmal vice does not exist. Or,
to be quite correct, it exists, but only for
export. When I landed I blushed to be a
human being; little brown-faced caricatures
of Egyptian monuments caught my coat at
every step, lisping half-English invitations to
every named and unnamed indecency. But
the next day I walked down the same streets
utterly unnoticed. Port Said has its dark
relaxations, but hardly more, nowadays, than
any other port of call. The old days of its
youth, when it was the sink of two worlds,
when you were knifed in the street, when
every white woman was a light o' love, and
every white man a bully — they are gone.
Port Said to-day is just coal and boredom.

III.

IN SEARCH OF THE EAST.

THE CANAL—ISMAILIA—THE EAST AND THE LEVANT—SUEZ—
SEYID MOHAMMED MUSTAPHA—AN ARAB MUSIC-HALL—PORT
TEWFIK—THE CANAL REVENUES—A FEAST OF COLOUR.

December 19.—One lazy, irrecoverable day
I had spent in the bawling streets of Port
Said, waiting for a ship to take me down
the Canal to Suez. Liner, freighter, or
dredger, it was all one to me, if only something that could float would let me aboard;
only, of course, ships came up and up, and
none went down. So this morning I rose
up betimes, wasted no minutes in the usual
mosquito-hunt, and got me to the shed
which Port Said calls railway station. The
little toy train of the Suez Canal Company
was just thinking of starting for Ismailia;

after all, I could see the famous Canal
from that.

I did see the famous Canal. For three
hours the train - tram never went out of a
walk, and all the time I saw the Canal.
Never, I suppose, has any single work of
man upset the balance of the world like
the Suez Canal; it has made and unmade
men, cities, nations. But to look at, it is
just a narrow ditch cut through a sheer
wilderness of sand. On the Asiatic side the
brown desert stretches away flat, empty,
endless. On the Egyptian a narrow ribbon
strives to relieve the aching barrenness with
a little green. A ditch of sweet water runs
between Canal and railway, and with its
aid a few dwarf trees and bushes struggle
above ground; but, even so, they attain
only to grey, not green. The Suez Canal
goes on mile after mile, unbending, through
desolation.

The same white and red buoys mark the
central channel; you pass the same grey,
patient dredgers, scooping up silt and spew-

ing it out, along what looks like a section of a broken suspension bridge, into its mother desert again. An ocean steamer hardly seems to move, for it must make no wash, lest the banks fall in; it looks as if it had strayed into a place too small for it, as a trout might look in a gold-fish vase, and could not find its way out again. The stations you pass are the abodes of the Canal officials, and nothing else. A few palms and cactus show above their compounds; a few natives light the eye with a blaze of blue, and yellow, and crimson garments. But the desert runs up to the very fence; that past, you are trudging the dead sand again.

At length far off, as the Canal widens to a blue lake, you see a mass of dark green. It is too big for a Suez Company bungalow: it is Ismailia. Pick your way through the black veils of women and amber caftans of children, who sit peacefully on the platform as in a waiting - room — and then you can refresh your starved eye with greenery indeed. Ismailia is all groves of yellow-beaned acacia-trees—the dust-brown stems twining bare and serpentine below, the leaves weaving into a thick canopy over-head. From walled gardens droop many flowers—white stars, scarlet buttons, purple cups. It is a little French town, well laid out, symmetrical, trim. It is almost too symmetrical, too trim to be real; it looks like a model Egyptian town, ready to go on tour. You could almost fancy yourself at Earl's Court—except for the emptiness of it. It was built on the new Canal to be a thriving town, a bathing resort, the half-way house to Cairo. But now it is only a place where you lunch on the way from Port Said to Cairo; it precariously supports a small population of railway porters. Ismailia is almost as dead as the desert.

It was a relief when the train came in for Suez. Up to now all I had seen was not the East, but the Levant: certainly the Levant has a charm of its own, but at Suez, they told me, I should find the real East. We rumbled

In a courtyard.

C

off through the drifting sandhills; presently
they opened, and we came into a stretch of
land, with palm-groves and a broad, sweet-
water canal, and cultivation; but dusk fell too
fast to see what it was. And a little after it
was only too certain that we were ploughing
the sands again. But at last I saw lights
ahead—many lights—and we were crawling
along broad streets with low, square-roofed
houses. Then a gabbling crowd bearing huge
lamps with the names of hotels on them.
None of your gold-laced dragomans or red-
lettered porters for Suez—just a half-dressed
runner with a big lantern.

Now at last I was in the East. I gave
my bag joyfully to a white-capped, white
night-gowned, bare-footed, chocolate-coloured
boy, and stepped forth. Another figure met
me at the gate—just such another Oriental,
and addressed me. Alas, in English! "Want
a donkey, sir; ride round-a-town?" It
was pitch dark, so I said I didn't. "Yes,
sir; you want donkey," he insisted; "good
donkey, sir, this donkey—good Jubile.·

donkey." And I thinking I was in the East !

And on the door of my bedroom I found my first Egyptian inscription. It was partly defaced and evidently very old, but I could

The tourist.

reconstruct the whole of it : " Travellers are informed that the proprietor is only responsible of values or things who are personally confided to him."

December 20.—After dinner I walked out

to see what I could see of Suez. Presently I
came up to a huge many-lighted house whence
pealed the joyous notes of " 'E dunno where
'e are." I learned afterward that this was
the office of the Eastern Telegraph Company,
which furnishes nearly all the English population of Suez; but at the time I wondered if it
was public and I might go in. As I stood
dubious in the dark, a neat tweed-suited man
in a *tarbush*—the Egyptian for fez—strolled
up and addressed me. I understood no word,
yet it sounded familiar; where had I heard
that language before? Then suddenly it all
came back to me; he was talking Dragomanese.
It is a language I speak very well, and I entered eagerly into conversation.

As is the wont of dragomans, he began with
a brief summary of his past life. His name
was Seyid Mohammed Mustapha; he was a
native of Suez, and his age was twenty-five.
He had been three years with an Italian gentleman inside Massowah, Red Sea, every place
between him together. "I go between that
gentleman together, three days' walking all

together, get alongside one place in that country, look round the corner, see if those people
go all in one line together, come all round
Massowah."

The translation of this is, that he had been
interpreter to an Italian officer, and had ac-
companied him in a reconnoitring expedition
inland. The rest of his harrowing adventures
on that occasion I forbear to tell; that history
was not his strong point I gathered from his
account of Moses. " Mozzes," as he called
him, in connection with a well he wished me
to visit, " he was one man—you not know
'im, sir ?—one officer, four, five hundred years
before, come between his regiment together,
all in one line, see if no water there. So this
regiment, sir, angry from this Mozzes."

But if he was a weak historian, Seyid Mohammed Mustapha was a true philosopher.
" Two things," quoth he, " are more best as
any other thing; one to keep three, four yards
from one woman—every woman. I bin everywhere; I know everything; I know when one
man not go near one woman, he feel beautiful

and fine, strong for himself. One other thing.
When I go to our mosque, I sit by the sheikh,
and he say, 'God say, Keep one eye on poor
man all the time—very nice.'"

The devout misogynist took me to an Arab
music-hall; I can hear the jangle and drone
of it in my ears still. Really, it was only a
double shop—blue and bluff plaster-walled,
cigarette-stump floored, furnished with a
coffee apparatus and benches. At one end
were the performers, squatting on a divan-
platform, raised about six feet; in front of it
was a deal rail, with a row of candles stuck
on to it by their own grease. The audience
was a jostling mass of every type and every
colour, except flesh-colour. The modern Egyptian is crossed, they say, between Arab and
ancient Egyptian or Copt, with a dash of
negroid Nubian thrown in. The faces of these
people illustrated the process—yellow, copper-
coloured, brick-red, chocolate, brown, black.
There a frank, thick-lipped, flat-nosed, woolly-
haired nigger; there an oval-faced, high-
cheeked Arab, white eyeballs gleaming out of

his dust-dark face and black hood; next to him a chocolate, round-cheeked, small-featured, genuine Egyptian mummy.

But however different they looked, they all enjoyed themselves vastly. Especially when there came in a lady dressed in a crimson velvet gown, with a brown skin insertion just below the waist, bangles on her ankles, many gold chains, and a huge silver watch round her neck, and began to dance. The band struck up—three men twanging strings, two women and two children lifting up a loud nasal chant. The music, to my ear, was one phrase over and over and over again; the dance, to my eye, a very slow methodical waggling of the belly, doubtless difficult to produce, but interesting mainly to the anatomist. But the yellow, and brown, and black faces went broad with grins, and their applause rose tumultuously above the screech of the smallest singer.

Next a young man put on a pantomime mask representing a bull's head, in which guise he performed shuffles for about three-quarters of a minute. He was salvoed with applause, whereat he at once passed round the head. On this there came in a stout young man with the face of a Roman emperor, only darker. "That very rich man," whispered Seyid with enthusiasm; "see what clothes he wear!" At first sight he appeared to wear only an old ulster and a greasy turban; but closer scrutiny indicated him as the one man in the room, except myself, with not only shoes, but socks. And underneath his clothes were all silk; this was a man indeed. Yet he was quite simple and unaffected; he fell easily on the knees of two friends, and called for some white spirit or other; when he got it he did not drink, but just made little pecking sniffs at it, as a lady pecks at a bouquet.

His fall propelled a negro in a red fez and blue dressing-gown into me, but by this time the fun was much too riotous to bother about a little thing like that. A black policeman came in, and made remarks interpreted to mean that this disorder must cease. He was

greeted with roars of laughter, slapped com-
panionably on the back, and escorted into the
street again. The twanging and the jangling
rose louder and louder, the lady's abdomen
twitched more and more abnormally, every
eye in the audience was rolling with delight,
every voice bellowing jokes or applause, the
very rich man was pecking faster and faster
at his liqueur. The Arab was enjoying his
Saturday night. I seemed to have stumbled
on a corner of the East after all.

December 21.—Quite right; to-day, for the
first and only day of my journeyings in Egypt,
has been spent in the East. It is queer that
the two ends of the Canal should be so utterly
different. Port Said is the Levant; Suez is
the Orient. Port Said is young; Suez is
very old—one of the very oldest surviving
towns of the world, a compeer of Damascus
and Tangier. Port Said is prosperous—at
any rate in the estimation of others—and
likely to be more so; Suez is quite done with,
and knows it. To be sure, Suez does a little
import trade in things like dates and Indian

fabrics, but it is very little. When they made the Canal, Suez supposed that her day was coming again, and began dock- and quay-building. Only the Canal passed her contemptuously by and joined the sea at Port Tewfik, nearly a couple of miles away, and Suez was left high and dry to look at silent quays and empty basins. Poor Suez!

From the railway station you see Port Tewfik, a cluster of green and white and brown. The railway embankment between town and suburb is an isthmus at high water, a streak across a waste of sand at low. I went down by train and found a clean and thriving little community — flourishing avenues, an esplanade along the Canal bank, white, gardened houses flying consular flags. It is plainly prosperous, only its prosperity is limited and artificial, like the prosperity of all the bungalows you pass between here and Port Said. They all live on the Canal dues. The Canal is practically a French colony forming the Eastern frontier of Egypt: as is the wont of French colonies, it is very full of officials, and could probably do with one-third of its present staff. However, the dues are high—very high : a big P. and O. liner will pay as much as £1000 for permission to go through. Not that the P. and O. objects : " keeps the little people out, y' know," it reflects with cheerfulness. But it also keeps out, among other things, Indian wheat for the British consumer. The Canal gets all the custom it wants, none the less — seventeen out of every twenty ships being British—and it pays. Its income you may put roughly at £4,000,000 yearly ; its expenditure at half that. Out of this it pays a handsome dividend to the shareholders. But what becomes of the rest of the difference between receipts and expenditure no outsider knows—though some whisper Panama. They hint that things somehow seem to cost more on the books of the Suez Company than they can ever be induced to cost in real life elsewhere ; that the little steam tramway carriages between Port Said and Ismailia run to almost double a fully appointed first - class coach on the

P.L.M.; that a simple flagstaff for signalling
has been known to get through a thousand
pounds. It sticks, say these cavillers—somewhere, somehow the money sticks. Be that
as it will, it is at least strange that the
Canal's British directors do British interests
so little good. A dozen years or so back
there were plans for a competitive canal;
only instead, the existing company took new
directors, gave them stock, and promised
certain reforms, such as doubling the width
of the channel and giving precedence to mail-
steamers. It promised, but nothing came.
It will not come in the lifetime of old de
Lesseps, said optimists—and it has not come
since his death either.

Then go down for the sunset to the stretch
of sandy loam they call the cricket-ground.
It is crowded with people walking up and
down—turbaned Arabs, or Greeks and Italians
with wives and children. All look down the
gulf, and look you down too, for such an
intoxicating draught of colour your Western
eye has never tasted yet. In front of you

shines the sapphire of the sea or the turquoise
of the sky; to your right, where the sun is
sinking behind them, the Egyptian mountains
loom black - purple under flame - orange and
liquid gold; to your left the mountains of
Arabia catch up the last rays and distil them
to a flood of rosy crimson. But what is the
use of naming colours? There are no names
for colours! Who shall say, for instance,
whether the African mountains are black or
violet, or does the dying sun—he is turning
to scarlet now out of flame, and the edges
of the scarlet are cooling to carmine—does
the sun take all the colour out of everything
else? You must see colours, not read about
them, and see them at Suez. So rich are
they, so pure, so gloriously intense, as if they
shone with their own light, a prism of suns.

That was colour; that was the East.

But never mind that. I am going back to
Suez, and as there is nobody looking, why not
take a donkey? Suez is decrepit certainly,
but it is very oriental — the last clinging
foothold of the East, now beaten out of

Egypt. The mosques here are more Indian than Saracenic in appearance — low, broad, white squares, with small domes set in the middle of them. In the bazaar they mostly talk their own languages and sell their own products — tin-ware hammered in a sort of cupboard rather than a shop, dates, big turnips, and fowls carried all day alive by the legs. For a town that is hopelessly played out, Suez is contented enough—perhaps all the more so that it is hopeless, **and need** make no more exertion.

IV.

IN SEARCH OF EGYPT.

GRAND CAIRO — SHEPHEARD'S HOTEL — THE BAZAAR — THE MOSQUE OF EL AZHAR — A PROFESSOR AND HIS PUPILS — THE MOSQUE OF MAHOMET ALI — THE PEOPLE — TOMMY ATKINS.

December 22.—Grand Cairo! And Grand Cairo, even after such towns as Port Said and Suez, is a bitter disappointment.

Port Said and Suez may not be much; they may amuse you or they may not; but, at least, they stand for something — the Levant and the East, and, whatever they are not, they are at least themselves. Cairo, on a superficial view, is not itself—seems to have no self to be. Out of your rather shabby first-class carriage, you alight in the gathering darkness at a rather shabby station of Conti-

nental type. There is the usual fight for your
body between hotels, the usual fight for your
baggage among porters. Then you are out
in a broad square, crowded with carriages,
donkeys, and people, and carpeted with two
inches of mud. The other side of the square
seems to be a dishevelled railway siding; its
centre a stopping-place for electric trolley-
cars. Then, before you know where you are,
you have driven through a couple of narrow
streets and you are at Shepheard's Hotel.

Inside Shepheard's Hotel you will find just
the Bel Alp in winter quarters. All the people
who live in their boxes and grand hotels, who
know all lands but no languages, who have
been everywhere and done nothing, looked at
everything and seen nothing, read everything
and know nothing—who spoil the globe by
trotting on it. And outside is the native
complement of them — guides and donkey-
boys, hawkers of matches and piastre toys,
rigged up in Bedouin garb as bogus as the
wares they purvey or—on commission—persuade tourists to buy, every variation of touts

D

and beggars clamorously waylaying their prey.

December 23.—Not but what Cairo has features clearly defined enough. It has its Levantine features in its dirty streets of retail shops, with their magniloquent signs in Italian

Street scene, Cairo.

and Greek—"Commerce Grocery," "Oilshop Confidence," and the like. It has its oriental features, which had grown old before ever a winter tourist set foot in Cairo. Also it has its Egyptian features — its pyramids, that looked down on this place before ever Cairo was, and when Egypt was neither Levant nor Orient, nor north, nor south, nor anything except the heart of the world. But these I have only seen as yet like sandhills in the distance ; they look from the citadel as if they were coming undone, but one must not pre-judge them. However, I have this day seen a bazaar, two mosques, a citadel, and the Abbassieh quarter — a beggarly morning's allowance for a sight-seer, but very fair going for a mere journalist.

About the bazaar there is little enough to tell. It has been much over-praised : not for size, completeness in itself, extent and genuine-ness of business, nor the mysterious effect of many colours in the half-light of numberless arches, is it fit to be compared with the Great Bazaar of Constantinople before the earth-quake fell upon it. It is a maze of narrow alleys, with open-fronted shops, full of all manner of cunning wonders—carpets, gold-embroidered silks, silver - embroidered cash-meres, gold and silver and chased bronze,

sapphires, and emeralds, and amber. Only
hardly any of them are made in Egypt, except
the sham antiquities : the best of everything
comes, or says it does, from Damascus, Constantinople, Rhodes, India—everywhere but
Cairo. And then you miss the stately, green-
turbaned, grey-bearded Turks squatting among
their merchandise ; instead, you are saluted in
lisping English and clipped French. The influx of the West has almost resulted in fixed
prices ; you can buy a thing in Cairo in some
ten minutes, where in Constantinople you
would play all the comedy of going away in
disgust, and being called back by a messenger,
and going away again, and dropping back by
accident, and taking a friendly cup of coffee,
and at last making your deal under protest on
both sides. Of course, you pay just as much
too much in the end ; but you have had your
bit of East thrown in.

If we want to find the Egyptian Egypt we
must walk on a little to something if not older,
at least more unchanging. Let us go to the

mosque of El-Azhar, the most famous seminary of all Islam, a university centuries older than Oxford or Bologna, a university which counts, even to-day, twenty thousand students. They are building a new front to the court; and once more there seems something almost grotesquely un-oriental in the idea of adding to or restoring an ancient mosque.

We must wait at the door till the sheikh brings us slippers, for the dust of the street must not profane the holy place. While waiting, observe the old, old man cruppen together in a bunch on the ground, a book on his knees, swinging to and fro as regularly as a pendulum till he dips his forehead in the dust. He is neither a professor nor an undergraduate : he has merely looked in for a little quiet devotion, to which Moslems consider the pendulum action peculiarly conducive. Now comes the sheikh with the great, flopping, lemon-coloured slippers, and we go in. Other devotees are strewn at random over the sun-lit court; some with their noses literally

scraping the lines of the Koran—for Egypt,
what with glare, and sand, and flies, and dis-
inclination to wash, is the home of blindness.

Now let us go into the mosque. A mean
mosque, you would say — lacking the noble
scope of the Sulimanyeh at Constantinople,
to say nothing of the perfect proportions of
St Sofia. Meanly furnished, too — matting
instead of carpet, with no shining candelabra
or gold - emblazoned names of God. This
mosque is small, oblong, and not very lofty;
the space is cut up by numberless pillars and
low wooden rafters, whence they hang the
lamps during the great Feast of Bairam. It
is no size, and you cannot see even what size
it is.

But the great feature of El Azhar is its
classes—and here they are. The whole floor
of the mosque is littered with them. It is
a profane similitude, but to me it rather
suggests Tattersall's Ring —the little dense
group round each expositor, and the babel
of many voices—except that here everybody

is sitting. The whole ladder of education lies before you. Here is an elementary class; little brown-faced rascals, their elder brothers' tarbushes down over their ears, are having cobwebby Arabic A B C's painted on tin slates by the grey-headed master. The classes run to no more than about a dozen apiece, which is just as well, for the master seems quite unable to control more than one child at a time. The others fight or laugh or try to get their feet out at the open necks of their shirts; and you cannot but reflect on the enormous advantage of the Eastern schoolboy, in that he can play in moments of tedium with his bare toes. Behind the next pillar you see the top of the ladder. A cross-legged circle of bearded young men, text - book in hand, are poring over some religious point which the half-blind professor monotonously expounds. I hope they are gaining profit; but if you contrast the dead stolidity of the graduates with the twinkling eyes in the A B C class, it hardly seems a testimonial

to the vivifying effect of the system. What
else could you expect? The education of
El Azhar is dead and deadening; education
in Islam is still in hand-and-foot bondage to
theology; what else could you expect?

Now, come up to the citadel, to the Mosque
of Mahomet Ali, the first Khedive, the Great
Khedive. Here was an Egypt — it was as
late as this century—not unworthy of Egypt's
past. These were the days when conquering
Egypt came within a march or two of Constantinople, and even so was only turned back
by the coalition of half Europe. The mosque
is the token of such a period. All is marble
and alabaster. You can wellnigh see yourself
in its flagstones; its bell - shaped fountain,
with cupola, all richly carved, speaks for an
empire in itself; its inside is majestically vast
and majestically empty — nothing but rich
carpets underfoot, and then, through the
shining candelabra, the names of God in gold
in Arabic and the mosaics of the dome above.
There is that in the solemn emptiness of a

great mosque which seems to stimulate a
large devotion far better than the niggling
trappings of a cathedral.

And now, come out of this regal tomb into
Cairo. Look at it first as you pass down—
what a great and flourishing city ! Look at
the huge mosques with their fretted minarets,
the dense brown and swarming dots of population in the native quarters, the lanes of
green and luxurious villas of the European
and Levantine suburbs of Ismailieh and
Abbassieh. Look across the ribbon of the
Nile where the great bridge strides over
it by Kasr-el-Nil barracks, and then leftward to the hoary Pyramids of Ghizeh and
Sakarreh, and rightwards to the royal palaces,
white jewels among their trees. You would
say that such properties alone, to say nothing
of the men and the edifices to-day, must surely
make a great and proud city.

But now come down and look at the people
of Cairo. There are the grandees of modern
Egypt rolling by in their London or Paris

built carriages — a flash of scarlet and gold waistcoats, white drawers, and bare, brown legs, as their running grooms shout to clear the way before them, and then a stout frock-coat and tarbush in the landau. These grandees are proud to call themselves Turks, or even Armenian. Here are the common people, squatting in little open shops, or driving donkeys, or doing delightful nothing in the sun. They are Arab crossed on Copt with a dash of Negro; who knows what they are? They call themselves Arabs, not Egyptians—and the clean-blooded Arabs disown them. And here is the Italian wine-shop and the Greek grocery; the interpreter with those American tourists is a Syrian, and he is expounding to them an official document issued in French.

No, no; there are no Egyptians, and there is no such nation as Egypt. And then the blare of a band swells up the street—

"When I were bo-und appre-entice in famous Lincolnshire"

—and khaki, white helmet, Lee-Metford and

bayonet, buckles and pipe-clay, swings past
Tommy Atkins. That is the first and last
thing you will see in Cairo that is all in one
piece and knows its own mind. That, for the
time being, is Egypt.

Street scene, Cairo.

V.

ON THE EGYPTIAN CONSTITUTION.

OUTWARD EVIDENCES OF ENGLISH RULE—A HEART-BREAK-
ING HANDICAP—A TOPSY-TURVY CONSTITUTION—KHEDIVE,
CONSUL-GENERAL, AND SIRDAR—FOREIGN CAPITULATIONS
—CAISSE DE LA DETTE—THE REAL GOVERNOR OF EGYPT,
THOMAS COOK AND SON—THE PROGRESS OF FIFTEEN YEARS.

December 24.—Egypt is very much like
Turkey to the outward eye; yet almost
from the moment of landing you begin to
notice differences. The general effect of
them is that Egypt seems to be being
governed; Turkey does not. At Port Said
you observe the coastguard and the police;
their uniforms are not merely whole, but
smart, clean, workmanlike. You go a little
farther and you see a man carefully sweeping
the street. A little farther a couple of men
are mending the tramway—squatting down

to do it in true oriental style, but the fact that they are mending anything at all is staggeringly un-oriental. As you travel about you notice that the railway carriages—that is to say, the newer ones—are comfortable, clean, and stoutly built; they bear the legend in English, "Boulac shops," with the date of construction. Each train has a post-van, an animal-van, and a couple of vans for fish and vegetables. The newer engines are well-set-up English-looking creatures: they have quality, as a cavalry subaltern well put it, unlike those underbred brutes, French locomotives.

When you get to a hotel, you are indeed asked for your name and dwelling-place; but not whence you came, whither you go, your vocation, religion, and all the rest of your biography, in which Continental Governments are so interested. The country is well managed, it seems, yet without fussiness. Even at Port Said and Suez, let alone Cairo, you find a well-worked system of telephones; such a thing could never be allowed in Turkey, for it cannot be censored, like the telegraph, and people might hatch treason over it. In Cairo, again, you find a well-worked system of electric tramways—and is it not a proud reflection for the Londoner that both in telephones and tramways Moslem Egypt, Arab Cairo, is ahead of his own Imperial city?

Of course, you know why it is. "England has got Egypt now," you cheerfully say, and think no more about it. But not quite so fast. England, as you say, has occupied Egypt ever since 1882; but if you think occupation means doing as you like, then you go the way to do great injustice to the men who are doing England's work in this country. They do keep things fairly straight, but the British newspaper-reader can form not the faintest idea of the heart-breaking handicap they run under. Egypt has the most topsy-turvy constitution in the whole world; and it is impossible to understand in the face of what prodigious difficulties we have done our work in it, until you have some vague notion exactly how topsy-turvy it is. So, if it is not too much of a bore, I will try to tell you.

In theory, Egypt belongs to Great Britain no more than Shepheard's Hotel belongs to me. There happen to be British garrisons in Cairo and Alexandria, but that is quite an accident. They are there to maintain the authority of the Khedive and to restore order. They have been engaged in these modest duties for nearly sixteen years now; Egypt is as orderly a country as exists on earth, and the Khedive, for one, would be only too glad to try maintaining his authority without them—only, somehow, they still stay. In practice, as everybody knows, they are there to uphold the paramount authority of England in Egypt : in theory they came there at the time of Arabi's rebellion, and have not yet gone away.

Besides the army of occupation there are two classes of Englishmen doing England's work in Egypt. One is the staff of the British Agency. Its head, Lord Cromer, is,

as you know, the mouthpiece of our policy
and, in practice, the ultimate ruler of Egypt.
They say in Cairo that when Lord Cromer
is feeling well, and well disposed to all the
world, he goes to the Khedive; when he is
not he has the Khedive to see him, and that
in either case the Khedive does what he is
told; though we must not pay too much
attention to what they say in Cairo. Only
in theory Lord Cromer is not even an
Ambassador, but just a Consul - General —
which means a gentleman who concerns himself with ships' papers and small disputes
between British subjects — and also British
Agent, which might mean anything or
nothing at all. In theory, he has no more
right to tell the Khedive what is, or is not,
to be done than you have. He just happens
to give advice, and the Khedive happens to
take it.

The other class of Englishmen is in the
Egyptian service. There is a financial ad-
viser to H.H. the Khedive, a judicial adviser,
English under-secretaries in the departments

of Public Works, the Interior, the Treasury, a
high official at the Education Office, and a
very resolute-minded Sirdar at the War Office.
In practice, these gentlemen are the adminis-
trators of Egypt. In theory, they are subordinates of the Cabinet Ministers, and the
Cabinet Ministers are subordinates of the
Khedive. The English under-secretaries
happen to suggest reforms, and their chiefs
and the Khedive happen to approve of them.

You will readily perceive that this arrange-
ment will work well enough as long as everybody wants it to work well; it is only when
they do not — which is usually — that the
position becomes a little complicated. But
as yet we are only at the beginning of
complications. If this were all, we should
only have Egypt to deal with. But Egypt
is only half or a quarter of an independent
country. There are in Egypt, as in Turkey,
what are called Capitulations with foreign
Powers, and the general effect of these is that
Egypt has hardly any jurisdiction whatever
over the subjects of any Power with which

she has Capitulations. These include all the
Great Powers and most of the small ones.
Practically, Egypt has no authority whatever
over the foreigners within her gates. She
cannot tax them without the consent of their
Governments, though they may make a for-
tune out of the country; she cannot punish
them, though they may commit every crime
in her calendar. If I were to go out of the
hotel now and shoot an Egyptian, and then
go into a Frenchman's house, the Egyptian
police could not enter the house without the
presence of the French Consul, and could not
arrest me without the presence of the English
Consul; and by him I should be tried. As
Egypt is chock-full of foreigners, many of
them the wealthiest men in the country, and
many also the most rascally, these Capitulations add a new perplexity to the task of
government. Since the occupation things
have improved slightly, in that foreigners
have now to pay one out of the three principal taxes; and of course they are always
to be got at by the 8 per cent customs duty.

The Greek courts, too, which formerly used to aid and abet their countrymen in all manner of crime, have lately become much more judicial. But with all that has been done, the Capitulations remain an ever-galling shackle on Egypt, and the Powers — which means France—show no disposition to knock them off.

And that is not nearly all. Not only may not Egypt punish those who commit crimes against its own people, but it may not even spend its own money. Before the British occupation Egypt was so ill-advised as to become virtually bankrupt. So in the interests of her creditors, the bondholders, Europe set up the Caisse de la Dette. On this body sits a representative of each of the six Great Powers. The revenue of Egypt is divided into two nearly equal parts: one-half goes to the Caisse to pay the interest on the debt, the other half to pay for the government of Egypt. If the bondholders fall short, the Government has to make it up. But the Government may be as short as it likes; the

bondholders will not help it out of their half
of the revenue, unless the Caisse unanimously
agrees.   As France and Russia are represented
on the Caisse, it need hardly be said it is
exceedingly likely not to agree.   The com-
plexities of this double budget are endless;
but perhaps we have had enough complexity
for one morning.   It is enough to say that
the interest on the debt is easily paid every
year, and that Egypt must go short of necessary reforms for want of cash; while the Caisse
out of its surpluses has piled up a useless
reserve fund of six millions out of Egypt's
own money, which Egypt may not touch.

The nominal suzerain of Egypt is the Sul-
tan; its real suzerain is Lord Cromer.   Its
nominal Governor is the Khedive; its real
Governor, for a final touch of comic opera,
is Thomas Cook & Son.   Cook's representative is the first person you meet in Egypt,
and you go on meeting him.   He sees you in;
he sees you through; he sees you out.   You
see the back of a native—turban, long blue
gown, red girdle, bare brown legs; " How

truly oriental!" you say.   Then he turns
round, and you see "Cook's Porter" emblazoned across his breast.   "You travel Cook,
sir," he grins; "allright."   And it is all
right: Cook carries you, like a nursing father,
from one end of Egypt to the other.   Cook
has personally conducted more than one expedition into the Soudan, and done it as no
Transport Department could do.   The population of the Nile banks raises produce for Cook,
and for him alone.   In other countries the
lower middle-classes aspire to a place under
Government; in Egypt they aspire to a place
under Cook.   "Good Cook shob all the time,"
is the native's giddiest ambition — a permanent engagement with Cook.

Cook gives no trouble; but the other prin-
cipalities and powers are not so easy to deal
with.   If France is sulky, she refuses to let
Egypt have money out of the Caisse reserve
fund for Egypt's most urgent needs.   If
Greece is petulant, she refuses to convict her
subjects of crimes, and lets them go assaulting
and burgling at large through Egypt.   If the

Khedive loses his temper—and he can be very naughty when he likes — he can incite the Englishman's official superiors to overrule his suggestions, or his subordinates to disobey his orders. And in all these cases, in theory, the Englishman is helpless.

And yet it works. Fifteen years ago Egypt was bankrupt, rebellious, miserable, oppressed, defeated. To-day she is solvent, orderly, prosperous, well-governed, victorious. For the next day or two I am going round in a carriage from office to office asking how on earth it was done. But one thing, meanwhile, is quite certain: England did it. Did it without especially intending it or altogether knowing it: did it, that is, by sheer unconscious English genius for rule.

VI.

HOW IT STRIKES A PASHA.

CHRISTMAS DAY IN CAIRO—THE ANTI-ENGLISH POINT OF VIEW
—THE CASE OF THE PROCUREUR-GÉNÉRAL—SIR JOHN SCOTT
—ORIENTALS AND WESTERN RULE—A HOSTILE PASHA.

December 25.—I woke this morning in the usual cage of mosquito-gauze, rang the bell, and the usual brown face under a tarbush poked itself in at the door. "Cold bath." "Allright." The Egyptian mind sees nothing familiar in "allright," believing it to be the English for "yes." The customary dialogue was now over, but the brown face remained inside the door. Suddenly it widened into a gleaming grin: "Good Christmas, sar," it said. By Jove! yes; it was Christmas Day; and looking out of window I saw, for the first time in Egypt, a true English sky—

heavy and yellow. It was chilly cold too but that it always is at night; Egypt is not near so warm as it looks. Looking down from the window, I started. Was I still asleep, or did I really see that great white bird, stork - billed, duck - footed, waddling placidly up to the back-door of Shepheard's? And then I remembered that a tame crane of great dignity was wont to disport himself there; but that took all the Christmas out of my mouth.

When I got up I found the hotel full of bouquets of roses; a few people went out later, ostensibly to church; but otherwise the wandering English made Christmas Day much like any other day. No such luck for the British residents. It seems that when they first came here, the society of Cairo was much concerned to find that they had no day for all going round calling on each other, as Continentals do on New Year's Day, Levantine Christians on their New Year's Day, twelve days later, and Mussulmans at Bairam. On consideration, the

society of Cairo decided that the British
ought to have such an anniversary, and
fixed on Christmas Day as the most suit-
able. The British had to bear it, and with
time it has grown to an institution. So the
ladies sit at home all the afternoon dealing
out tea, and the gentlemen go round, calling
on everybody else, and Egyptian friends call
on everybody after the same manner; so
that the whole British colony, with native
auxiliaries, rotates in a body round itself all
Christmas afternoon.

A stranger, I was called on for no such
effort; so I went out peacefully to lunch with
a pasha. There is something very piquantly
un-Christmas-like in such a recreation. My
pasha, to look at, was quite European, all
but his tarbush. His face was really large,
but looked small because of the keen alert-
ness of every feature; he was really of the
middle-age, but his sharp nose, twinkling
eyes, and hair, showing close-cropped when
he pushed back the tarbush, gave him almost
the aspect of a boy At table were his

daughter and her English governess — the Englishwoman precise like a governess, but open-minded like a woman who has seen the world; the daughter, with great black eyes in a pale face, double pigtail, dressed much like an English schoolgirl, demure beyond her years. After lunch — just elaborate enough to be excellent, but not so elaborate as to be ostentatious — we talked politics. And I very quickly perceived that my pasha, a personal friend of many British, was no friend of Britain in Egypt.

"I am in opposition? No; I am no longer minister, but here, unhappily, there is no opposition."

I said I had gathered that, one way and another, there was a good deal.

"Yes; but what is it?" he cried. "Here there is no party government, no constitutional government, no public opinion. Here we must sit and obey our masters."

"Then would you like to see us go tomorrow?" I said.

And at that he went off: he pushed his

fez furiously backwards and forwards over
his bullet head, and broke forth uncontrol-
lably. "Would I like all my servants to
leave my house to-morrow? What should
I do? If all you English went to-morrow,
what could Egypt do? It would be ruin.
The English are everywhere; every good
post must go to an Englishman; how is it
possible that the country should govern itself when only Englishmen are allowed to
govern it? You say you are here for our
good; you are teaching Egypt to govern
herself. Teach her by all means, we say.
But what do we see? At first it was only
a few English in the highest positions; good.
But now the second-rate and third-rate positions are filled by English too; each year
there are more. It seems that the longer
you stay here, the less able are the Egyptians to govern themselves. You are not
teaching us, and you are preventing us from
teaching ourselves. The other day the Procureur-Général was turned out of his office;
he is a poor man, with many children; an

Englishman now takes his place. And it is
not an English office — Procureur-Général;
the English are not used to the duties. Yet
an Englishman! Fifteen years' occupation—
and there is no Egyptian fit to be Procureur-
Général. Pouf!"

The case of the Procureur-Général moved
his indignation especially. I do not pretend
to know the merits of it, but this is what I
had gathered. A few weeks ago an Arab
journalist, you may remember, was imprisoned
for libelling the Khedive. The ingenious
author printed an Arabic ode in slanting
double columns: if you read it at one angle
it was a glowing panegyric, if at another it
came out slightly otherwise.

" All hail, great Prince !
        Whom I can only call a calamity to this country."

That was the general trend of it, and it
must be owned that, if libelling monarchs is
crime, this was a clear case. But it is said
the Khedive seized the occasion, with the
help of the Procureur - Général, to go for

everybody he disliked, though there was no
jot of evidence to connect them with the
libel. The Procureur-Général, so went the
story, was told he mustn't do things like
that; whereto he replied that he was acting
under higher orders. Whereon he had to go.

But my pasha would hear of no apology for
such an act. "The people see a high official
removed like that, with no trial, nobody
knows why; they say he is a victim—it is
because he opposed the English. It is very
easy to talk of unwholesome palace influ-
ences — it is fashionable nowadays — but I
do not believe it. He was removed because
he did not do what Sir John Scott told
him. This is not teaching people to govern
themselves; it is introducing funk."

"I suppose Sir John Scott was his official
superior," I said; "I should call it introducing discipline."

"But such a high official! With smaller
ones, certainly; otherwise, no government
would be possible, but a Procureur-Général!"

"All the more, we should say in England."

"But he is dishonoured; things are said against him, and he has had no trial."

"But if he is considered a victim, then how is he dishonoured? And if he is innocent, why doesn't he defend himself publicly?"

"Ah, he is a poor man; he has many children; he might lose his pension."

"Pity he didn't think of that before he disobeyed orders."

"But a Procureur-Général! You would surely not expect the same implicit obedience from such a high official! A Procureur-Général!"

And so on. The case of the late Procureur-Général is doubtless more interesting to himself than it is to me. But I quote this bit of conversation to show the unbridged gulf that yawns between the Eastern and the Western mind. Here was a gentleman of perfect manners, high education, and great experience of business of state, travelled, speaking many languages perfectly, and excellently acquainted with the affairs of all Europe. But to him it appeared monstrous that a high official should be cashiered for insubordination as if he were a low one; and the size of the man's family and its proportion to the pension seemed to him vital merits of the case. Is it a wonder that Orientals do not understand Western rule?

Still, from the pasha's point of view, the argument that Englishmen are taking more, instead of less, part in the Government from year to year, thus preventing natives from trying their hand at ruling, must be admitted to carry its weight. "Presently," he said, "you will have a popular uprising against you. Formerly it was only the upper classes who were discontented; now, as Englishmen take second- and third-class posts, it will be the bourgeoisie and the peasants." He also asserted—wrongly, if I remember the figures—that the land-tax has not been reduced, while prices have fallen heavily. Also, that our presence makes France jealous, and disposes her to lock up Egypt's money in the Caisse reserve; which, from Egypt's side, is undoubtedly a point. Also, that the difficulties of Egypt, which culminated in Arabi, were really due to European interference; also, that the British had not done very much for the country, most reforms really dating from the Dual Control. These two arguments tend to kill each other, but no doubt there is a foundation for each of them. Pending inquiries into all this, I left my hospitable, excitable, England - hating pasha ordering his carriage to make Christmas calls on his English friends.

VII.

AN ARABIC EDITOR AND BRITISH TRADE.

THE KEEPING OF DIARIES—THE NECESSITY FOR A SENSE OF
HUMOUR—THE WORLD'S HALF-WAY HOUSE—A COSMOPOLITAN
BAR—THE INTERIOR OF AN ARAB NEWSPAPER-OFFICE—AN
EDITOR'S VIEWS—A SCIENTIFIC JOURNAL—THE WANT OF
BRITISH CAPITAL AND TRADE.

December 29.—I notice that all the dwellers
in Shepheard's Hotel keep diaries except me,
who am paid for doing so. You can see them
in the writing-room, jotting notes on large
sheets of foolscap, or entering the finished
product neatly into neat leather-bound vol-
umes. At *table d'hôte* you will hear them
quoting from the same works — sometimes
even producing the book itself to guarantee
their reminiscences. For my part I have long
repented my rash undertaking to keep a diary.
Here are four days since Christmas and not a

F

line of entry to show for them. I wonder what I have been doing!

Not much, I am afraid, fit to put into a diary. But I have knocked about, and I have discovered a certain number of things. I have started a circular tour round the Under-Secretaries and Advisers of Egypt with a view to discovering how on earth they keep Egypt going; but it progresses slowly, because the only public office the Cairo cabman knows is the War Office, and he always takes you there first, to inquire your way to somewhere at the other corner of the city. In my Cairo of course—the sun-seeker Cairo—they do not know what Government offices are.

I have also taken all the expert opinion I can on the general political situation, beginning with the donkey-boy outside the hotel and winding up with Lord Cromer. Lord Cromer has been playing Christmas games at the British Agency, and the Levantine-French editor of the little piastre rag which impotently reviles him has been sitting up till one in the morning at the *café* talking high politics:

which is Egypt all over. Working men sit
playing backgammon in the streets at midday,
and schoolboys get up at one in the morning
and read lesson-books till five; that is just
Egypt. For a man with a sense of humour
transcending work, worry, anomaly, obstruc-
tion, and summer-heat, Egypt must be a paradise; of a man without this it must soon
break the heart. You must laugh or die.

Add that it is the half-way house of the
whole world : that you meet this man on his
way from Borneo to Rio de Janeiro, and that
going out from Boston (Mass.), to shoot a
black panther in Sumatra; that English Masters of Arts keep American bars, and United
Presbyterians work hard at their offices on
Sunday—and you will own that Egypt is a
piquant country enough. The men that have
been broke, the men that have been disbarred,
the men that have cheated at cards, the men
that have done nothing in particular except
not get on with civilisation — you will find
them between ten and early morning clutch-
ing brass rails before the bars of Cairo.

Where two or three are met together it is
odds on that one of them has changed his
name.

And what do you say to this for social pic-
turesqueness?   I went into the St James's bar
yesterday afternoon: at the door a wind-
burned Arab face looked out of a white hood
and offered to guide me to some snipe-shooting.
Inside the bar was a fat-faced young native in
a shepherd's plaid lounge-suit, talking the
English of Piccadilly to the barmaid.   The
man outside was no more a Bedawin than I
am; he was one of the imitations who hang
about the Pyramids with fierce looks, and
blackmail timid tourists for backsheesh.   But
the man inside really was a Bedawin—a Bedawin chief; not one of whose people except
himself had ever seen a town.   And he had
been educated at Haileybury!   And beside
him sat a prince of the Khedivial house
standing Scotch whisky to a British sergeant!
The man was half awed, half patronising; the
prince was half condescending, half propitia-
tory, and he was saying how much he admired

the English. Can there be any place in the world like Cairo?

But we must remember our politics, and here even politics have their piquancy.

For example, I went the other day to see the editor of an Arab newspaper. His office is a disused palace: all new Khedives and their relations build new palaces in this country, so that it is difficult to find a house of any size that has not begun life as a palace. In the middle wing sits the editor writing his leader—a string of Arabic cobwebs down a narrow slip of paper. The editor is a stout man in tarbush, blue serge, and yellow elastic-sided boots, with two warts on his nose, and a deep blue dimple on his chin; he writes in a light overcoat and a rug over his knees, for it is a very cold winter—clouds half-way over the blue sky, and you must shut your windows by five.

He has just finished a slip of copy: he rings a bell, and there comes in a little brown-faced devil in a tarbush, blue gown, bare brown legs, and slippers. "May you

see the office? Of course"—and out we go
to the left-hand wing of the palace. Here
are about six bare rooms, all open to the
others, the plaster peeling here and there from
the high walls.   Here stand the cases of
curly Arabic type—bigger than ours, because
the language has more symbols: here are
the bare-legged compositors at work.   In the
next room the paper is going to press on the
old-fashioned sort of machine; as the white-
turbaned, brown-legged, white bicycle-skirted
native turns at the wheel for his life, the half-
printed sheets swing slowly over, one after another, a maze of twirls and dots and quiggles
that you would say no man on earth could read.

And not many can.   The sub-editors can,
of course—four grave-faced young men in the
inevitable tarbush and overcoat, solemnly
translating from the 'Times': they salaam
respectfully, and when the Englishman, who
looks as if he had plenty money, returns their
salute, as being brother journalists, it sur-
prises them much.   "But," says the editor,
"our circulation is as large as any in the

East, but not large enough to necessitate a
rotary machine: yet we sell five thousand
copies daily; it is something in a place like
this. It is difficult: other native papers are
subsidised by France or Turkey or others;
we, because we are independent, must shift
for ourselves. Still it grows and grows: our
paper is read in India and Somaliland."

This seemed to me the opportunity to find
out the native view of things in Egypt, and
I began to ask questions. Remembering my
discontented pasha, I asked whether there
was any native feeling to the effect that there
were too many English officials and too much
taxes. He said there were many Englishmen
in the Government certainly, and no doubt
the people would say that they would rather
not have foreigners; but, for his part, he
didn't think there were too many to do the
work. As for the taxes, they have gone down
near a million since 1882, but they are still
very high for a poor country. They do not
work out the same everywhere, but in some
districts they come to 40 per cent of people's

whole income. Try that in England! And on the top of it prices are falling here, as everywhere else: nobody's fault. Last cotton crop stood for a loss of something like three millions as compared with the year before—and that in a country whose total budget runs under eleven millions on each side. And until the Khalifa is smashed at Omdurman the army will want every piastre, money will still be scarce, and things will not loosen—unless England helps.

"Then there is another thing," proceeded the editor. "I do not think you do enough for native education. In two ways you might help it. First, in the way of helping primary education. I think it would be well to give a small subsidy to deserving teachers in primary schools, who are very poorly paid. And secondly, it would be well to subsidise scientific journals—not political, you understand, but purely scientific and intended for popular education."

"But is there any such thing in Cairo?" I asked.

Orientals do not blush red; but I could see my editor blushing inwardly as he replied. "Yes," he said, ingenuously; "we have one such of our own. Here is a copy of it."

Of course I couldn't read it, but if all in it was as good as the list of contents it must be a useful and deserving publication indeed. It begins, of course, at the back, like all Arabic works, and then breaks out into an illustrated jubilee article on progress during the Queen's reign, with an incidental sketch of the whole history of European culture, and adorned with portraits of the Queen and her Prime Ministers. The blocks would hardly be taken by 'Black and White,' but all the same Lord Rosebery is plainly distinguishable from the Duke of Wellington. Then follows a translation of a paper read before the Smithsonian Institute, a brief essay on the Moral Ideal, and a paper on crystals. Then comes the Family Doctor, with simple prescriptions for various complaints, the ladies' page, warning the fair against deleterious aids to beauty,

and the answers to correspondents desiring to
know anything from the best way of taking
stains out of silk to the solution of a theorem
in geometry.   In short, it has everything for
the learned as for the learner; and when sub-
sidies to popular scientific journals begin in
Egypt, I make no doubt it will receive the
most favourable consideration.

The editor had been frank, both in his criticisms and in his hopes.   But he did not at all
imply by what he stated that our rule in
Egypt is a failure.   On that point he was
very clear.   "It is now possible," said he,
"that a fellah should bring a lawsuit against
a pasha and win it.   Before the occupation it
was unheard of.   The taxes may be high, but
everybody knows that he pays only what the
Government orders.   A man who has money
is not afraid to use it, instead of pretending
to be a beggar.   The people would never consent to go back to the old order of things.
There is — how do you call it? — there is
security."

Then the mention of money brought him on

to a point that was evidently a keen one with him. "Why do not the English invest money in Egypt?" he asked. And indeed everybody here asks it. Foreigners are buying land, either for their own cultivation or to let. Natives are buying land, for Mussulmans are forbidden to lend on usury: they creep round the prohibition often by taking their interest in produce, but land is their best investment. It pays 8 to 10 per cent, and you are as sure of getting your due in Egypt nowadays as you are in England.

Yet British capital goes neither into Egyptian land nor any whither else. The Cairo electric tramways are Belgian, the gas is French, the water French and Government, the railways French and Government. Nothing British except Cook and one narrow-gauge railway. There are not six British shops in Cairo. "Why do you not do it?" asked the editor again. "It would do good to Egypt, which has no capital of its own; it would do good to England by increasing her influence in the country. And it is good business. Will you not say that to British investors?"

I told him plainly I had little influence with British capitalists, but that I would mention it; and I hereby do. I do it with the more confidence in that I find the matter referred to in Report No. 391 of the Foreign Office Miscellaneous Series—a monograph on British trade which every British trader would do well to read twice. It can be bought either directly or through any bookseller for 2½d., and that being so, I am not going to waste my time and yours making an abstract of it. It tells the usual weary story—foreigners content with smaller profits, excessive rates of commission charged by English agents, unelastic terms of credit, incompetent travellers. We are ahead of any other nation, it is true —well ahead; but our lead is not increasing. In all other ways our work in Egypt may make all of us proud, but the British trader is not making the most of his chances. Government would be glad enough to accept British tenders; only often they are either

too high or not according to the specifications,
or else they do not come in at all. It seems
that we—we with pinched manufacturers and
workless workmen—are too proud to take the
trouble to supply the sort of things that
Egypt wants. We ought to remember two
things. First, Egypt is Eastern in that it
wants things cheap; not too good, but just
good enough for their purpose. Perhaps it
ought to want the very best : only it doesn't.
Second, if Egypt is Eastern in its require-
ments, it is Western—while England is here
—in its integrity. As the editor says, there
is security.

VIII.

WATER.

THE FIELDS OF EGYPT—WHAT THE NILE IS TO EGYPT—THE
BARRAGE—THE CULTIVATION OF LOWER EGYPT—HISTORY OF
THE BARRAGE—THE RESERVOIR AT ASSOUAN.

December 31.—Br-r-r-r! This the land of
sunshine! As the omnibus train jolted out
of Cairo I shivered in my long overcoat. The
other passengers in the long, second-class
carriage—it was a Government carriage, and
it was like a rejected cattle-van fitted up
with worn-out seats from a third-rate village
ale-house—were shivering worse than I. Is
not this the coldest Egyptian winter within
the memory of man? Sitting on the little
platform outside the carriage was a black-
veiled woman, with a child arrayed like a
rainbow; propriety would not allow that she

came inside with the men, and how she shivered I should not like to think. From time to time there passed along the train a shaggy Arab selling bread.

The train limped rheumatically at about a couple of miles an hour through the fields of Egypt. Nobody could call Egypt a beautiful country, but nobody could deny that it is a picturesque one. Under the steely clouds green and brown fields stretched out on either hand. They were all split up into tiny squares by tiny embankments and tiny ditches now dry; tinier ditches still ran along each furrow. Here and there was a native hoeing or pulling turnips or washing them; here and there a little blindfolded fawn cow was treadmilling round a creaking water-wheel, raising water by an endless chain of earthen buckets, all leaking more or less—some with holes through their bottoms. Presently you would pass a group of palms encircling white, low houses, with what looked like a thatch that had been put on with a pitchfork, but was really the inhabitants' store of dry brushwood fuel. The country looked poor, but very fertile.

I was going to see the reason of its fertility. At last the train laboriously stopped at a platform with "Barrage" written up. I found myself accosted by two boys with a trolley: "You belongs Mr Joseph, sir?" they were asking. Mr Joseph was the engineer in charge of the Barrage, and for the moment I did belong to him. So I sat on the trolley, and off they went at a pace which would have lost the train. Presently we ran under a castellated arch, and the Nile appeared — the ancient Nile, floating grey and stately, not hurrying itself, between low, yellow banks. We were out on a bridge now — a broad bridge of many arches, with yellow stone parapets. Then we ran on to the land again, and beyond, just after a shorter bridge over a broad canal, was just such another long, parapeted bridge over the second great branch of the Nile.

Nothing very much in that. But presently

the engineer came out and began to tell me all about it. A good man was the engineer to look at—broad-shouldered and lissom, with a straight, resolute, British face, as carefully shaven as if he lived in Piccadilly. No shoddy nor backsheesh, thought I, and no red tape either, when you get Englishmen of this stamp at work. And then he began to explain; but to explain altogether I must go back to the very beginning.

Egypt is the Nile. That is no epigram or figure of speech : the street I tread on in Cairo, the beef and potatoes I take for lunch — they are just solidified, organified, vitalised Nile. Every rod of tilled land in Egypt was washed hither from the Abyssinian mountains, and laid down to fertilise the desert, by the Nile. The great river not only gives water to a rainless land, it makes the very soil. If the land is hardened by the brown, mud-bearing water each flood-time, it will bear well; if not, it will soon go back to desert again. If the water is not drained off after flood-time the flat land

will become waterlogged. And if the full
Nile should burst its banks the land will
become a lake. The Nile is Egypt's all in
all — to be trained and cockered, filled up
now, emptied out then, coaxed into giving

The banks of the Nile.

the greatest possible life and leaving behind
the least possible death. Egypt is, of all
others, the land of the engineer: he makes
or unmakes it, enlarges or diminishes it, according as he succeeds or fails in managing

the Nile. The British engineers in this country are making it—quite literally and visibly and palpably making Egypt.

The Barrage is one of the greatest pieces of Egypt-making in the country. When you come to walk over it, and look back on it, and down from it, and up at it from jutting piers, you see that it is not the big bridge it first appeared, but an enormous dam, with locks and weirs. In each arch are a couple of gates, one above the other; they are raised or lowered by a travelling-winch on the parapet above. The water can be passed under, or over, or between them, regulating the Nile. Regulating the Nile means regulating the Canals. East and west of the Barrage, and from its apex between the Rosetta and Damietta branches, take off three great canals; each makes a province. When the river is high the gates of the Barrage are opened, and let off the water down its natural channels; when it is at its lowest, in early summer, the gates are closed, the Rosetta and Damietta estuaries

go all but dry. The life-giving water is
held up at the Barrage, and turned into the
Canals.   You only realise what a river-by-
itself the Nile is, when you understand that
one of its chief functions is not to run into
the sea.

To understand better, you must know that
there are two systems of cultivation in Egypt.
In Lower Egypt — that is, the Delta — and
one district of Upper Egypt the land is
watered by what are called summer canals;
in the rest of the country the land is watered
and manured together by letting the flood
Nile over it.   On this system, fields can be
cultivated only in winter, when the water
runs off them, between the flood and the
drought.   Lower Egypt is cultivated all the
year round; sugar and cotton, which require
water in plenty but yet in moderation, can
be grown, and two or three crops of vegetables raised in a year.   The Barrage has
given the necessary water for these crops;
and you will see the benefit of it by the fact
that, since it has been working, the cotton

crop alone has gone up from a little under three to well over six million hundredweight annually. Think what that means — more than doubling the yield of the country. If we had done nothing else in Egypt at all we should have justified ourselves by this work alone.

But credit where credit is due; the conception and first building of the Barrage are due to a Frenchman—Mougel Bey—in Mahomet Ali's time, nearly sixty years ago. Only it took twenty years to make, and even then was not finished; only the Rosetta half had been used, and you can see the curve in it to this day where the vast structure bulged before the pressure of the water. For the Barrage rests on a poor foundation of fine mud and sand; it has an artificial floor and aprons of masonry; still, under all is only mud and sand. So, in 1883, the great work was officially declared worthless; and then came along Sir Colin Moncrieff and his men, and doubled the wealth of Upper Egypt with it. But it is still a daring work, and its foundation is still mud and sand, and the man who has the nursing of it has an anxious life. Of course, the French pray for its bursting nightly, and prophesy it weekly—only, it has not yet burst. At high Nile springs appear beneath it; as I walked along it we came to a gang of natives vociferously working at what looked like a drill right through the bridge. They have made holes right down through the piers, and pressed in cement until what went down one came up at another. So now it has a solid floor, it is hoped; and the Caisse de la Dette has advanced money to build a couple of weirs below it, which will halve the head of water on it. It is too vital to Egypt even to chance a break-down.

All this about the Barrage, because it is the biggest and the most beneficent and the easiest to see with your own eyes of the good things which England has given Egypt. Her gifts have been many—internal peace, justice, honest administration—but water is the best gift of all. In the old days, before we came,

there was not so much water; which means
there was not so much Egypt. What there
was was turned on to benefit the rich, on to
the Pasha's fields and the Governor's; the
poor man had to wait and see if there was
any left when they had done. Nowadays he
knows that while there is a drop of water
he will get his fair share of it. And water
is the one thing he wants, for it means crops
or no crops, wealth or ruin, life or death.

The irrigation of Egypt is not finished yet.
There is still a vast deal to be done, especially
in the way of drainage. It is not enough to
bring water to the land; it must be taken
away again. Land can be made out of desert
by water; but there is also much that can
be made by drains out of swamp. Before the
British engineers took things in hand Lower
Egypt either had no drains, or it was a hopeless tangle of unfertile drains and fertilising
canals running into each other, and cancelling
each other's work. That was Egypt all over.
Now new drains are being made everywhere,
and old ones siphoned under canals they

empty into. Large areas of salt marsh, especially round Alexandria, are now good land, letting well and teeming with necessary supplies for the great port. There is plenty more marsh left to work on. It is a work of time, and it is a work of money—and only when you know how tight money has always been in Egypt can you appreciate the work of Sir Colin Moncrieff and Sir William Garstin and their men. Only money is all right just now; in two years the Caisse — perhaps a little ashamed of its close-fistedness about the Dongola campaign—has granted out of its idle reserve nearly a million for irrigation and drainage. Egypt's money could not be better spent for Egypt's good.

One more great work remains — the projected reservoir at Assouan. If the Nile could be held up and stored there, then Upper as well as Lower Egypt would rejoice in two crops a-year, sugar could be produced enormously, the cultivable area of Lower Egypt once again vastly increased; above all, the very possibility of water famine

would be done away for ever. The plan
has been considered and approved by a capable international commission. Only the
reservoir would cost five millions. It would
pay Egypt over and over again, and the
Caisse de la Dette has an easy five millions
of Egypt's money. Therefore, because the
project is British, would be executed by
Englishmen, would constitute yet another
British boon to Egypt — France says no.
That — you would hardly believe it of a
nation which remains great, in spite of con-
tinual efforts to be small—that is France's
Egyptian policy.

IX.

AN EGYPTIAN ETON.

IN THE PLAYGROUND—THE PRIMARY SCHOOL—A COMICAL CLASS
—MARRIAGE IN THE SIXTH STANDARD—AN ELABORATE
SYLLABUS—ENGLISH v. FRENCH—SCHOOL DISCIPLINE—THE
ANNUAL SPORTS—THE EFFECT OF IT ALL ON THE EGYPTIAN
BOY—CHRONIC DISHONESTY.

January 2, 1898.—They were training for
the sports. In the sunny playground was
a row of big, fat boys—though none of them
came within six inches of the slim, young
tarbushed English headmaster—hanging on
to a rope made fast round a tree. The
trained instructor from Aldershot—he was
not so young nor slim as he had been, but
with muscles all india-rubber and steel—
was teaching them the tug-of-war. His
white-toothed, black-faced, khaki-clad Soudan-
ese assistants were helping him. "Down,"

he cried, and swung on the rope as it
tautened. "Up," and it slackened again,
and then he pointed out where they mis-
applied their force. They all understood
his English. A dense semicircle of boys in
tarbushes and overcoats, standing solemnly
round looking on, all understood English, too.

I was in the Egyptian Eton. It was one
of three schools originally founded for training teachers capable of giving instruction
in English or French. But now it contains
primary and secondary schools, and a training college for the teachers; so that I was
in a fair way to see at its best a summary
of the whole system of public instruction in
Egypt. It is only in its infancy as yet;
and if you read this through you will have
some idea of the difficulties that beset it.

First we went into the primary school.
There were not many pupils, because the
fees in this school are high — as much as
£12 and £15 a-year for day boys—and nobody comes to the primary part except
those who have failed elsewhere, and whose

fathers think the high fee a guarantee of
high cramming. The primary course in
Egypt takes four years : in the first, only
Arabic subjects are taught; after that, English or French is introduced, and gradually extended till in the two last years it
takes thirteen hours out of the weekly,
thirty - three. All the instruction in languages is given in the language itself, but
by natives. Only one — English or French
— is taught, but that is supposed to be
taught thoroughly.

The examination for the primary certificate
is held in three centres—Alexandria, Cairo,
and Assiut—besides which there is a special
centre for pupils of the military school. This
certificate qualifies its holders for the secondary schools, and the lower appointments in
the Civil Service. To get it you have to
pass in Arabic, your foreign language, arithmetic—only four sums, but one must be in
money or weights and measures — writing,
and geography. None of them are very
alarming ; yet a most astonishing number

of candidates contrive not to pass. In 1893 the proportion of the successful was hardly 1 in 3—342 out of 936. The teaching they get from their native masters is not over good; all the same, the fact that so many are ploughed is rather promising than otherwise. It shows that the examination is not a farce, and yet the numbers entered for it increase from year to year.

In the lowest class there were just four boys — absurd little owls with the gravity of old men, dressed in tarbush and overcoat: they were getting a drawing lesson from an elderly Arab with a shawl round his head; when I went in they all stood up and saluted. In the highest class they were having an English lesson from a young native in a large butterfly tie. Their English was thick and sloppy; so, if it came to that, was the master's; still, you could understand it. In this class moustaches were already budding, and it seemed strange to hear young men reading infantile stuff about the sparrow. You are not surprised to find that the syllabus for this class includes "Politeness in conversation. Visits. Society functions."

The great difficulty in schools like this arises from the fact that a Mussulman is never a boy. As soon as he leaves the harem — often already corrupted by the women—and is no longer a baby, he jumps at a bound to being a man. A boy will do well in his classes up to fourteen, fifteen, sixteen; and then suddenly the *cafés* and hashish and mistresses claim him—and from a bright-eyed urchin he becomes a sallow, flashy, sodden, stupid, dissipated man about town. In one primary school two boys, sixteen and fourteen, have just been married— not betrothed, you know, but really married, and living with their wives; the native master saw nothing extraordinary in a married sixth standard boy. Under the former system a boy took his primary certificate at fourteen or so; then spent six years getting his secondary certificate, and then perhaps went on to the training college, or the schools of medicine, or of law. Consequently he might easily be the father of a very fair-sized family years before he started to earn a piastre of his own.

Lately, by shortening the secondary course from five years to three, a real effort has been made to get boys out of hand and into the world before twenty or so. When we got on to the top form of the secondary school there was no appreciable difference in the sort of boy. They were all young men, and not apparently less young at eighteen than at fourteen—all tarbushed, all overcoated, most moustached, all grave, as if school were a matter of life and death. The studies of these upper primary classes are a good deal more ambitious than those of the primaries. The secondary education certificate is necessary for everybody who wants to enter the higher Government schools, such as those of medicine and law, or to take any tolerable position in the Civil Service. Therefore it is worth working for. For their secondary examination they take up Arabic, English, or French, arithmetic, geometry, and

algebra, geography and history and science.
I was well educated once, but if these Arab
boys learn all the syllabus tells them to I can
only say they know a deal more than I do.
They know—or should know—all about the
mensuration of a right cylinder and a right
cone, their Euclid extends to Book Six, and
they solve—or not—quadratic equations. As
for science, they seem to know all about things,
such as sulphur dioxide, that I never heard
of. Still, if the scheme is a bit extensive, it is
sound also : in English they give special attention, for example, to the formation of nouns,
verbs, adjectives, and adverbs from each other,
and to the commonest prefixes and affixes—
just the sort of thing in which the native
usually goes wrong. And the history they
learn in their third year is all within the last
two generations — an excellent example to
many schools in England.

In fact, the scheme looks so thorough that
you would expect the candidate to go down
like ninepins before the examination. So they
do sometimes : in 1891 only 28 out of 128 got

through ; in 1892, only 36 out of 90. But in the examination preceding these evil years 115 passed out of 199, and since then the chance of passing has again risen a point or two above evens.

An interesting feature of the returns — which, as you will have perceived, I do not possess for the last few years—is the proportion of boys who take up English to those who take French. The school, you must know, is divided into English side and French side. There is a good deal of rivalry between them ; so much that when a French boy became good enough for the football team, the whole fifteen —all English boys—went to the headmaster and respectfully protested. He was an exceedingly immoral boy, they pointed out, and they would rather not play with him. As it happened, he wasn't an immoral boy at all—a great deal less so, in fact, than many of them—but that was their way of demonstrating the corporate spirit of the English side.

Now it is alleged by many that the British have failed to take any root in Egypt, and

that this is demonstrated by the fact that
Egyptians do not speak English, but still,
after all the years of occupation, prefer to
learn French. If you look at the figures of
the examination for the Secondary Certificate,
they seem to bear this theory out. The proportion of English to French boys during four
years was 38 to 161, 22 to 106, 15 to 75, 16
to 60. But the figures of the primary examination do not bear this out,—195 to 378,
and 337 to 599 are the latest proportions I
have. And an inspection of the books of the
Egyptian Eton backed these figures up. At
first the predominance of pupils leaned enormously to the French side. But as the years
have gone on the French numbers have
slowly dwindled, and the English slowly aug-
mented. To-day they stand as near as possible equally.

The difference to-day is less numerical than
social. The best-bred boys, the sons of Pashas,
are on the French side. If you go into the
dining-room—or rather the dining-rooms, for
the two sides eat apart—you will find that on

the French side they understand the use of knives and forks and spoons, and do not throw their bones under the table. On the English side it requires a perpetual struggle to prevent young Egypt from committing such atrocities. But it is only natural that the Pasha, who was brought up to consider French the official language of civilisation, who has himself talked French all his life, should send his son to the French side. But the poorer man, whose son must make his own career, sends him to the English side. It is nowadays the more useful language—and therein lies the answer to the criticism that we have not succeeded in Egypt because Egyptians still speak French. If we had been French or German or Russian, we should have made them learn our own language. Being only English—the owners of loyal French Canada, and half-loyal Dutch Africa—we do not enforce our own language, but let them find out the utility of it for themselves. We are in no hurry; we are not going away; and time is on our side.

There is no difficulty in point of discipline

with the Egyptian schoolboy; the French masters have some trouble sometimes, I was told; but in the very, very rare cases where an English master finds his classes too much for him, he must go: it will not do to bring up the young in the idea that they may set at naught the authority of an Englishman. Corporal punishment is not allowed by the Education Department—most foolishly, you would say, since it is the one punishment which really appeals to the young Egyptian, and it is the one best suited to his peculiar besetting vices. Instead, you will see a couple of sad-faced young men, in short frock-coats and long purple shirt-fronts and green ties, standing up while their fellows are at dinner: these Reguluses are on bread and water, but they feel the position so keenly that they prefer to go till evening fasting. An even extremer torture is prison, which consists in sitting a few hours in an empty bathroom. But the oriental mind sees no hardship in sitting a few hours doing nothing; and the penance leaves an offender hardened with whom

a good thrashing would be an abiding influence through life.

The only occasion when the Egyptian
schoolboy gives trouble is at the annual
sports. Here he is insubordinate indeed.
When the first meeting was held many eminent persons were invited to see what the
Egyptian schoolboy could do; doctors were
furnished by the Education Department to
tend the exhausted competitors on their arrival at the winning-post — only unluckily
they did not invite the mounted police. The
eminent persons duly came; so did five thousand Cairo schoolboys, for the meeting was open
to all Cairo schools. The half-mile was duly
covered in three minutes fifteen seconds—but,
alas for the behaviour of the five thousand !
They had come to see, and they meant to
see; they evaded or overpowered the police,
stormed the grand stand, and came swarming
over its railings on to Lord Cromer's toes.
The Under-Secretary for Education went for
them wildly with a stick; the English masters
present lashed out like men; one of them

unfortunately made a slight mistake, and
gave the eldest son of the Minister of Education the worst gruelling he ever had in his
life. Since then several powerful squadrons
of mounted police have always attended the
annual sports.

And what, when all is said and done, of
the Egyptian schoolboy? Does he do any
good in return for the patient, intelligent,
honest care his English masters bestow on
him? Well, he is learning to play football,
and that will be good for him; only when a
boy says to his master, after playing the
Egyptian Sandhurst, "The ground was too
undulating; it recalled to me Hannibal's pas-
sage of the Alps"—why then you perceive
that even football will not necessarily turn
a precocious man into a boy again. He is
astonishingly industrious; the difficulty is
not to make him work, but to prevent him
from overworking: eight hours' home work,
after five and a half in school, is by no means
an unknown performance. Some of his work
in English literature, which I saw, compares

quite well with that of University Extension
students at home; but, like theirs, it reads
very text-booky. He has an astonishing gift
for languages, and he can appreciate a play
of Shakespeare with ghost or witches in it,
and a good allowance of florid metaphor, no
worse — perhaps better — than an English
schoolboy. To the top class of the secondary
school I was kindly invited to put a few
questions. They were reading Shakespeare's
'Henry the Fourth,' and I started them off
on "Harry, thy wish was father to that
thought." Not one of them could give an
explanation of the metaphor that would have
satisfied an Englishman — and yet they all
understood it perfectly well. To the Eastern
minds, you see, such figurative language
was the inevitable way of expressing one's
self, and it would be much more natural to
translate prose into poetry than poetry into
prose. Only when I went up to the Teachers'
training class and started them on 'Hamlet,'
I saw they had enough of it. I happened to
know what "unhousel'd, disappointed, un-

anel'd," meant; so far I was a professor.
But rashly I asked one skimpy young man
whether Hamlet was really mad or not.
"There are three theories," he began. And
I collapsed.

But at the end of it all the Egyptian
schoolboy is parrot-like in his unintelligence,
incorrigible in his inaccuracy, hopelessly fatu-
ous in his dishonesty. He understands ordinary English, if you ask him questions, un-
commonly well; but he will reel you off a
page of text-book, understanding the mean-
ing of each word, but without an idea of the
connected sense of it. It is all one to him if
he writes + or — : it is only a difference of
one stroke, and why should the pedant of a
Westerner bother which he puts? He fudges
freely in examinations, and fudges most
clumsily. At a recent examination three
boys all brought in little cribs, consisting of
tips written on their blotting-paper. They
were discovered, of course, and hauled before
the head. The first said : "I missed a lesson,
sir, in consequence of ill-health; and to fix

it in my memory I wrote it down, and acci-
dentally, sir, the paper came on to my desk
to-day.   It is true, O sir; by God it is true!"
The master gently pointed out that one does
not write ordinary notes on blotting-paper,
nor can blotting-paper move on to a desk by
itself. But the other two told exactly the
same lie in exactly the same words. They
knew that they would not be believed; they
knew that they would be punished more
lightly if they told the truth. But they
only repeated, "It is true, O sir; by God it
is true!"

Will they ever make a boy of him? If
skill and trying can do it, they will; and if
he can be made a boy he can be made a man.
But it is work against the collar, and it will
not be done to-day or to-morrow.

X.

A DAY IN THE DESERT.

AN ARAB HOUSE—"GOOD ALL RIGHT *HEGIN*"—A SEA **OF SAND**
—A GUIDE AT FAULT—LOST IN THE DESERT.

January 4.—The camels were kneeling down
on the road outside the village. Half an
hour before I had awakened on the floor
of the best room of the richest Arab in
the place — the house white and solid and
stately from the outside, unplastered mud
walls and unglazed window - holes inside —
native Egypt all over. I went to the door,
and all but walked out—into nothing. Over
the doorstep was a sheer drop of twenty
feet into the yard, where cows, donkeys,
dogs, and men pigged together in the dirt
of content. The way down was to screw

yourself round the left-hand doorpost on to a flight of stone steps : in front of the best room — "Some day," said Said, "we are going to make another room there" — was only vacancy and a few loose, rotten beams, on which the skinny fowls live in mid - air. In front was some more of the village — fine plastered houses where it could be seen from the road, a maze of unbaked mud, dead walls, and blind, meaningless enclosures where it could not. But beyond that, again, was an embroidery of palm-trees against the flush of dawn.

By the time we got down to the camels, over the heaps of rubble, through the broken walls, across the field of springing clover, past the white figure on a carpet kneeling and bobbing towards Mecca, over the tilting planks that bridge the Canal where the women were dipping water — by that time everything was swathed in the grey morning mist. The camels were kneel-ing down, and we climbed on, side - saddle. Then a furious heave backwards, a hurl forwards, a milder pitch backwards again, and the beast had unjointed its legs and was going.

They told me the action of a camel—and especially a running camel, a *hegin* — spelt sea-sickness; but really its walk is not very much rougher than a rough-actioned horse's, its trot is much the same, only a trifle more so, and its pace for travelling is an amble. These were running camels, for we were going forty-five miles into the desert to a Coptic monastery, and no baggage camel could do that in the eleven hours of daylight. These were the genuine dromedary —"good all right *hegin*," said Said They wore a petulant, supercilious, half-vicious, half-petted expression, carrying their heads very high and very far forward, as if they disliked the smell of everything and everybody, but more especially of themselves. But Said said they were all right *hegin*, and I was happy.

As we swung out on the dusty road the great brown rugged Pyramids appeared

towering above us : then the mist cleared,
and the sun caught them, and another
pyramid, less solemn, laughed in the deep
blue water of the Canal. We turned sharp
to the right on to the sand, and left behind
us the smoke that said the Mena House
Hotel was beginning to boil water for the
bedroom cup of tea. We plashed steadily
through the bare sand, marked with un-
numbered tracks of all the camels and
sand-sleighs and donkeys of a Cairo season.
Then striking out through a little defile
between sandhills, the tracks all suddenly
left us. The sand hardened under the
camels' feet, and we were out in the desert.

Out in a new world — a world of sand.
The flat, deep-green fields, the flat, white
houses, the streaks of blue Canal, and the
grey, rolling river of Egypt, were clean
gone, as if they belonged to another world.
This world was all yellows and browns—all
sand. The braying donkeys and the bawling Arabs had floated away into the land
of dreams, and we had entered into the

land of silence. Mile after mile, hour after
hour, the camels swung on through sheer
sand and silence. It was not without form,
for the sand was banked up into low ridges,
little round hills, smooth slopes like sand-
drifts, long-rising glacis, steep-sinking gullies;
but it was without life. Here and there
the broken dints of a gazelle-track, now and
again the dotted hole of a jerboa's burrow,
once the shining skull and thighbone of a
dead camel. These came at intervals of an
hour; but no gazelle, no jerboa, no camel
did we see: the whole day I saw one bird,
and no other living thing save ourselves.
Only sand, sand as limitless and as barrenly
changeless as the sea — now darker, now
brighter; now clear, now shaded with basalt
pebbles; now a foreshortened rise to the
sky - line twenty yards ahead, now a prospect of a couple of miles of heave and dip
—but always sand, sand, sand.

We knelt down, and dismounted twenty
minutes for lunch — no more, for daylight
must be economised if we were to make our

goal by dark. *Heyin* carry riders, not burdens. Our stores had all gone on before by
a baggage-camel, to the monastery, with the
hegins' fodder; after lunch we had but a
half-pint of water between two white men,

Laden camels.

the guide, and the barefooted camel grooms
who toiled after us all day.

We were off again through the aching
desert. As the sun got up to its strength
the sand glared into my eyes till there was

nothing to see but a blur of sand. I looked
between my camel's small ears, over its con-
temptuous nose—high up as if ignoring me—
and saw only desert. I looked at a sandhill
eastward, then turned and saw it again westward. Far away on the horizon I saw a long
grove of dark-leaved trees, with a break in
the middle showing clear water—only I knew
there was no such thing. The monotonous
lilt of the dromedary's amble ran one thing
into another: they no longer had any out-
lines or perspectives, distances, shapes, or
colours. Before, behind, right, left, the whole
borderless desert was a swimming confusion
of sand.

I began to feel sleepy and droop in the
back. I swung my leg over the pommel and
settled to ride astraddle; at the end of an
hour I decided I would sit side-saddle on
the off-side for another hour, then change
and ease the strain again. So on I rode,
on, on, looking steadily at the great yellow
blotch before me. Presently I began to ache
again : it must surely be the hour and time

to change over. I pulled out my watch—
and it was just eighteen minutes.

But by now the sun was dipping down
again under our hat brims. By now Said
had dismounted from his flagging beast; his
white linen kilted up round his loins, he was
making casts to left and right, running up
every little hill and shading his eyes for
intense searching looks before and about him.
It was long past three; it was past four.
It would be dark at half-past five; if we
had not sighted our monastery by then we
were helpless. We must have come the
distance if we had come the way.

The eagerness with which the guide raced
up each new eminence, the strained hope-
fulness of his stare, the slow disappointment
you could read in the relaxed limbs, the
fresh hope renewed, but each time fainter,
with which he dashed for the next prospect
—he was at fault. To my eye one ridge,
one dip, one hill, was exactly like every
other. And by now the camels were jaded,
and the sun was down over the rim. We

had been riding ten hours, and must have
come fifty miles; our monastery was only
forty-five. We had missed it, and it was
all but dark. Under a bluff of loose sand
we halted the camels and dismounted.

A night in the cutting winter wind of
the desert, a night without tent, water, fire,
or fodder, was the very best we had to look
forward to. The worst—but just as the mind
strayed round to the remote possibilities up
panted Said.

"Have you seen, Said?"

"Effendim, I have seen; I saw from the
hill back yonder; come and see for your-
selves."

And he led us to the brow of the bluff,
and there, surely—yes, there gleamed something white. The monastery; hurrah! It
can't be four miles off; we will walk, and
the camels can follow. So up got the patient
camels, and off we strode, five miles an hour,
over sand as hard and crisp as the early
morning snow.

We walked. Now the sand grew softer,

now it hardened again, now it was shingle; but we walked fast, and we seemed to walk straight. The blazing crimson and orange of the sunset blinded our eyes to the white blob of the monastery, but by now we must be almost on top of it. Faster and faster we walked and walked. Now crimson and orange blazed no more; it was really dark now; we had come five miles; we had not arrived.

"Are you sure you saw, Said — quite sure?"

"Effendim," replied Said, "I thought I saw something white."

Nothing white in sight now. The guide was thrown out utterly: in that tangle, where you could never really see two miles ahead, you might as well have groped for a button as for a building. And there we were, fifty-five miles from home, camels done up and foodless, camel-boys starving, thirsty, and waterless, selves with possible two days' food, and certain less than one day's water —lost—clean lost in the Libyan desert.

XI.

A NIGHT IN THE DESERT.

THE CAMEL'S REAL CHARACTER—THE DESERT WHITELEY—A
CAMEL-TRACK—ILLUSIONS OF THE DESERT—THE MONASTERY
AT LAST.

January 5.—Often enough I had been lost
before, only this was different. In the desert
you can laugh at little privations as long as
you know the way—but once miss it in that
unanswerable enigma, that pitiless perplexity
of sand, and you have this choice before you.
You know that your Nile lies, perhaps, forty
miles due east of you; only, will your camels
—Pyramid picnic camels, untrained for the
privations of long desert journeys—will they
hold out, foodless and waterless, till you strike
it? You know that your monastery is, perhaps, within a mile, almost certainly within

a dozen miles of you—only dare you use up your beasts, and provisions, and strength hunting for it? That was the agreeable question we had to sleep over.

But the first thing to do was to sleep—though I, for one, felt a kind of prompting to walk about all night calling aloud for the monastery to come and pick us up. Yet that was soon forgotten in the new interest of the desert. During the day it was merely a thing to be crossed, a thing to be looked at —with interest, certainly, but with the sort of interest one gives a stranger. Now it was become more than a stranger — a friend or enemy, as the case might turn out, and all its moods and tenses were worth attentive scrutiny.

And, first, although the desert can be hot at midday, even in January, it can be bitter cold at night. I had never thought of the desert as a place in which to wrap up warm and get out of the wind. However, there was not very much wind, by good luck, and a sand slope under a semi-

circle of small basalt boulders gave bed and
shelter.

Said and the camel-boys disdained the slope
and the boulders, which led up to the next
point of enlightenment—the camels. Up to
then I had not appreciated the camel. These
were bad camels: one, as I should have told
you, gave out after half a day, and another
was threatening to kneel down every stride
before dark: but at its best a camel has none
of the generosity of the horse. When he is
called on to work he makes a noise something
between a dog's snarl and a peacock's screech;
while he is at it he wears an air of sulky
superciliousness, as who should say, "I'm
doing it, but not for any love of you." Also
at this season of the year he has a disgusting
habit of blowing parts of his inside out at his
mouth—a great pink bladder, which he puffs
out and sucks in again in the filthiest way.
But now I noticed that when the camels lay
down in the wind the Arabs carefully lay
down on the lee side of them. There was
no fodder, but they pulled up yesterday's

dinner from somewhere in their insides and
placidly ate that over again.   Somewhere else
inside them was a cistern containing the day
before yesterday's water, of which they took
from time to time a refreshing pull.   He may

Camels at rest.

be unattractive, the camel, but in the desert
he is the right beast in the right place.   He
carries his stores inside him; his body furnishes a vehicle by day and a house by night.
When there is no wood but petrified wood—

very like the thoroughgoing inhospitality of
the desert, is the fact that it petrifies its
wood—his very dung makes fuel. Bless his
ugly heart! He is food, drink, travelling,
lodging, and firing all in one—the William
Whiteley of the desert.

And then the desert is beautiful—cruelly
beautiful, but very solemn and mysterious.
When I lay down black night had dropped
over the limitless waste of yellow; we were
moving in a thick but partly transparent veil.
When I first got up to walk myself warm here
was a new desert—a desert of tender blue.
The white moon rode overhead; it seemed to
be staring close into your eyes. And now the
desert was no longer limitless. Its boundaries
had closed in round us; we were in a quarter-
mile circle of blue light, with soft blue curtains all about us. Behind them you knew
the pitiless expanse was there; but the circle
of light and the ring of shadow made us a
bed-chamber in the middle of it. It felt
somehow kindlier, more home-like than it
had done by day.

Yet again, when the moon had gone down, there was yet another desert. The chamber had grown smaller, and the hangings were changed to dark grey. There was still the black island of the camels, ever champing at their yesterday's dinner; but ten yards beyond the thick shadows muffled all else. They were thick, but not quite impenetrable; and though you well knew there was nothing living beyond, you half expected to see something loom up through them. Once I thought I heard the yap of a jackal, but it was only the hissing wind licking down over the sand - slope. The desert might advance or withdraw its frontiers: we were still always alone in it.

The next time the grey was different—the pale no-colour that waits breathlessly to get its life from the dawn. Now the east was reddening. Get up, Said, and let us use every instant of the light. A mouthful of cold tinned ration; but you can't eat much on a dry stomach. We will strike north-east; we may drop on the monastery, and, anyhow, that

should bring us on to the great desert road to
the Natron Lakes, while the camels last. But
Said—true Arab, though sham Bedawin—begs
for half an hour, just one half an hour, Effendim, to search again north-westward. Weakly
we give in to him, and off north-westward we
go again. Slowly as yet, for the sun is not up
enough to see far by, and we may as well spare
the camels. Soon Said is a dot racing along
the leftward sky-line, lost now, reappearing
half a mile farther on, sanguinely searching.

Then the sun comes up — steps bodily up
over the horizon — and the desert is yellow
again. And now—what sound is that? Yes,
a yell from Said. Surely he has seen. On to
the camels and briskly westward.

"Have you seen, Said?"

"No; but behold — a camel track, and I
know this place."

And then presently we come out on a wide
prospect—sandhills left and right, but in the
middle a vista over rolling miles of sand.
"See, Effendim!" cries the triumphant Said—
and there—yes ; it certainly is a bit of white,

it surely must be the convent. Forward then briskly; it is about an hour and a half. Forward we go, an hour, an hour and a half, two hours: we have been low down and could see nothing; now we come up on to a ridge again.

And the bit of white? Gone! Vanished away. There are three bits of white now, each vaguer, each more distant than the other. O curse this merciless, mocking desert! Three hours wasted, three hours of thirst for the boys and exhaustion for the camels—and we twelve miles farther towards Morocco, but just as hopelessly lost as ever.

Turn about north-east; we must get back now or never. On and on; try to keep a good pace without driving the camels. The sun is well up now; the desert is beginning to get hot—and very thirsty. But hulloa! What is this? A broad camel track with the prints of the naked feet of men. It looks as if an army had gone over it, so thick is it with footprints. Where does it lead to, Said? Said doesn't know: he has left off now even pretending to be a son of the desert.

"I think, Effendim," says the oldest camel-boy, "it leads to a village."

"What village?"

"I do not know."

O, wonderful mind of the Arab!

However, it leads north by east; along it we go. The latest tracks cannot be over two days old from the camel-droppings—maybe one; they went with baggage-camels, a long line abreast, and the men walked beside them with sticks. We may overtake them, and, anyhow, they were not going nowhere. Yes; here is their last night's camp, a ring of marks on the sand—one, two, three, six, ten, fifteen camels. Forward again! An hour later a couple of bits of wood stuck along the line of the track: that is a desert sign-post. Now, up over this brow—and there is a broad valley before us. "Know it, Said?"

Not Said!

But suddenly the camel-boy points to yet one more white speck, and a sheet of pale-blue. "Wady Natrun," he shouts. Why, yes, it surely must be; the blue is the Natron

Lake, and the white—well, we don't believe
in white spots any more, but the monastery
cannot be far away. Once more we go on
briskly under the spur of unquenchable hope.

Half an hour; an hour. Are you going to
mock us once again, torturing desert? The
white is white faces of sandhill now, and the
pale blue is growing slowly, remorselessly into
white also. But the white must be surely
salt or soda, and we must surely be coming on
to the trail.

"Effendim!" It was the smallest, ugliest,
silentest camel-boy that saw it first. There,
on the left, as we open the northward part of
the valley! A long, low, white wall—not a
blotch this time, but a solid wall with ends
and top and corners! We have arrived; no
thanks to anything except the merest luck,
but we have arrived! Forward, now, *hegin*,
to your fodder—the third is hopelessly behind,
lying panting in the sand; but what does
that matter now? There is the tall, brown
baggage-camel with the stores. Inside the
dead white wall are many wells.

XII.

A COPTIC MONASTERY.

A SILENT BUILDING—THE GUEST-CHAMBER—THE ALLURING
CIGARETTE—THE POSITION OF THE COPTS—BEDAWIN ATTACKS
—CELEBRATION OF MIDNIGHT MASS.

January 6.—It stands all by itself, far
out in the desert. North-west of it runs
a twenty-mile valley, with a string of salt
lakes, a village or two of semi-Bedawin, and,
in these latter days, a soda factory. When
first the brethren of St Mark came there—
a hundred and fifty years, men say, after
the birth of their Lord—there was nothing
but a few wild savages and sand. It was a
long day's journey from anywhere; there
was not a blade of grass within thirty miles
of it. It stands all alone on the slope of
a low hill of sand. As you approach it you

see one tree—stunted, and dry, and dusty,
but a living tree, a grateful wonder in the
desert—and a few ruined walls of the many
brother monasteries that once stood beside it.
Besides that, not a dwelling, not a patch of
cultivation, not a beast. The face of the
building you approach is a blind, worn, white
wall,—not a door, not a window, not an
embrasure even. In the dead silence of the
desert the convent seems as dead and silent
as all else.

On the other side is a sort of blue, wooden
hatchment bearing a cross; but still you
wonder how you can get in. Only as you
come opposite it you see that this cross
stands over the door—a stout, wooden door,
that the shortest man must stoop to go
through, half underground. The bell rings,
and presently a deep voice behind the door
cries out something in Arabic. "Pasha
Inglesi," is the reply. The door goes back
with a creak, and there is a small, brown-
bearded, blear-eyed man, in black burnouse
and turban. He salaams, and puts out his

hand, takes yours, and bows down and kisses it. You go in, and find yourself facing a dead wall again : turn to the left and go a pace or two, still between high, dead walls. Then to the right—and what is this?

It had looked like a tomb outside; now you are in a little world—a tiny patch of the world you know transported into the midst of the world of desert. The high wall was the wall, not of one building, but of a little colony : here are grey - plastered houses, brown mud cells, little white-plastered domes, pale-green palms; here—most blessed sight of all — is a deep, damp well, and a tiny patch of rich green clover. This world was vocal, too; you heard the caw of crows, the cooing of pigeons, the cackle of hens, and once the low of an ox. The outer wall —here crumbling, there fast and square— rose up high above it all, cutting into the brilliant blue heaven ; outside it was death, inside it life. The holy men had renounced the world, and left it; but they had brought with them just enough of it to live on.

They took us into their guest-chamber—without glass windows, but new, well built, large, and clean : it was added a few months ago precisely for the entertainment of strangers. Mattresses lay in the corners, and they seated us on chairs. The abbot, a stout, black-bearded little man with a twinkling eye, squatted cheerfully on the floor against the wall. Then a lay brother brought drink—a coarse, brown-gowned, un-shaven, dirty-fingered lay brother with the features of a convict and the grin of a schoolboy. Sherbet and coffee he brought —the sherbet was sickly, but it was cool and wet!—and we repaid with cigarettes. The fathers partook gladly and smoked furiously, dropping their ashes and spittle unaffectedly on the guest-chamber floor. They brought us black bread and stewed citrons and treacle and cheese. It was their Christmas Eve—old style—and they extended to us a cordial invitation for midnight mass.

It was the great ritual day of all the year, and I could not help feeling how much Mr

Athelstan Riley would have enjoyed it. All day long the tinkle of little bells and the boom of big ones summoned the monks to one ceremony or another. Nevertheless, the holy men, allured by cigarettes, kept dropping in continuously all the afternoon. We had put a chair against the door, as it would not shut, but that was no bar to their curiosity. A measured tread up the stairs, a grating at the door, and politeness demanded that I should spring up and open. Then in came the black, turbaned figure with a salaam, sat down on a chair, and stared methodically at us. Now it was the abbot, now a sort of sub-abbot, in a violet turban now the Newgate Calendar lay-brother, now a sack-clothed workman employed about the place. My companion had not much Arabic to spare, and I had none, except the word for "cab," which one can hardly use much by itself in a desert convent; so that conversation was not brisk. They sat and looked at us methodically till they had earned the cigarette, and then, without a word, went solemnly away. Nearly all of them were blind, or half-blind, or getting blind, not so much from over-study — one brother could nearly read Coptic, but he represented the whole learning of the foundation — as from ophthalmia, the scourge of Egypt. With the learned monk, who also knew a word of Italian, we did indeed hold a long, if vague, conversation, and got so far as to offer him whisky. He declined, regretfully, on the ground that it would spoil his voice for the night's chanting; but cheerily added that he would come in for it after twelve.

Pending that, we walked round the monastery, and a strange, pitiful tale it told, eloquent of many centuries' oppression. As a sect, the Copts, I suppose, are some seventeen hundred years old; as a race, some nine thousand; out of which, what with their own rulers and foreign lords, they have dared call their souls their own during the last fifteen. Their maintainable rights date from the British occupation; and only

the other day a native schoolmaster, in one
of the chief Europeanised schools of Cairo,
spat in a Copt boy's face, and called him
an infidel dog: the Copt father was too
tame even to prefer a complaint. So this
monastery wall was high and thick, and
offered no windows to be shot through. The
gate was secured by a wooden bolt of the
thickness of a man's thigh. And by the
side of it lay a big millstone; there used to
be two, and their use was this. When
raiding Bedawin appeared, which they did
perpetually, the monk on watch descried
them from the parapet. Thereon another
monk below rolled the millstones between
the lintels of the door, which they fitted
exactly. Then with pulleys—they are there
to this day at the top of the wall — they
hauled the monk up into their fortress. And
the Bedawin found it difficult to burst or
burn the gate across the millstones, and
difficult to pull the millstones out, for they
were wedged as in a vice.

If they did succeed in passing the door

there was a further refuge left. I went up
a flight of steps and then across a wooden
drawbridge into the great solid tower. There
are bits chipped out of the masonry as from
glancing shots fired against one of the small
windows. Within this tower is a well, a store
of grain, and two chapels: here the monks
could satisfy all their simple needs, and here,
with the bridge drawn in, they could tire
out the hostility of all the Libyan desert.
All over this queer outpost of Christianity
the maxim "Watch and pray" is written
very literally indeed.

But by now it was ten o'clock, and the
big bell was clanging for the great ceremony
of the year. We went down into the court,
guided by the hoarse monotonous cadence
of a chant. Through a low door we stepped
into what seemed a stable; then turned to
the right, and we were in church. It was
low and small, crossed by wooden beams,
and dimly lighted. On the flagged floor of
the outermost precinct lay heaps of grain
and sacking; within an open woodwork

screen stood the monks; beyond them, through a narrow door, we could see darkly into a farther round room with a table, about which moved three priests. In the middle partition was a carved wooden altar, curiously like a sideboard with china shelves above it; over that hung an antique picture with three gilded saints.

The monks stood, facing all ways, before lecterns; with the three in the inner chamber there were about a dozen. One old man followed, by the light of a crooked taper, the lines of an illuminated prayer - book, which he held an inch from his eyes; he had his back to all the others. Two more stood back to back. The lay - brother was kneeling with his face towards the outer chapel, where he stood. Another, his face muffled in his shawl, lay in a heap in a corner. Many supported themselves with a long crutch under the armpit. The whole place was fragrant with incense, and rang with the loud, nasal, perpetual repetitions of the chant.

The abbot took a triangle from a shelf, and beat it in time with the music. A priest came out of the inner room swinging a censer; he passed, swinging before each worshipper, till he came to us; as he paused before them, each bowed to his knees. Next the abbot and another, standing nose to nose, were intoning a duologue. Then the lay-brother took up a solo: it was plain he could not read, and had not the faintest idea what he was saying; as he halted and stumbled, deep voices from here and there prompted him, lest any word of the ritual should go unsaid. Now a brother was carrying forward a tray of small bread-cakes for consecration — the five wounds of Christ pictured in the middle, a Coptic inscription round the border. Then a priest from the sanctuary opened a cupboard in the wall, and took out vestments. In the dimness the innermost three could be discerned robing themselves round the table. The chant, which had drooped, broke out again, full-throated, almost furious. " Kyrie eleison;

kyrie eleison; kyrie eleison," it rang clamorously all round the dusty little chapel; it
floated out over the black, silent desert.
Then it hushed suddenly. From the holy
place came forth the priests in tarnished
vestments, but white and gold and scarlet.
Each of the black, muffled figures bowed to
earth before them, and greasy lips, in a
humble ecstasy, kissed dirty fingers.

XIII.

TAMING THE DESERT.

January 8.—I left a virgin page in my diary
last night because (*a*) it was too cold to hold
a pen; (*b*) I was teaching the new Swiss clerk
at the rest-house how to make (1) cocoa and
(2) toddy; and (*c*) by the time he knew toddy
it was one o'clock, and I had to get up at
half-past five.

I am back now from the four days in the
desert, from the scorching sun, and the biting
wind, the sand, and the vastness, and the
mystery, to find Shepheard's like a rabbit-
warren, and me consigned to an upper garret,
without room to swing a cockroach. To the

throng of fresh sun - seekers I will make a backsheesh of the Pyramids, and the mosques, and the bazaars, if they will only leave the desert free till I come to Egypt again.

Yet, if I ever come again to immemorial, ever-changing Egypt, I shall find a vast difference even there. British energy is transforming and civilising even the desert. Twelve miles from the monastery of St Mark stand the long, low, mud-and-board quadrangles of the Wady Natrun soda-works. You approach it by a string of deep blue undrinkable lakes and bulrush swamps, salt and soda frothing up like snow through the damp mud—less monotonous, but almost more desolately inhospitable, than the raw sand. You see a few tumble - down, wooden huts, and a shaggy Bedawin tent or two; you lick the salt off your lips and dried-up mouth, and wonder how their inmates do not go mad with thirst.

Then you come to the factory, and there rises up before you an Englishman, who asks you, by way of introduction, to have a drink. The sort of Englishman that is made in the

waste places of the earth, late of the Bechu-
analand Police, burnt brick-red, eloquent, not
in speech, but in every strong, self-contained
movement of his body.   He has been here
alone with blacks and Bedawin for nine
months, and will be another year with a
German clerk; but he does not grumble more
than every Englishman everywhere: he just
stays at his post, and shoots, and rides, and
gives orders.   In the clean - boarded mess-
room he set us down, and fed us, and told
us all about it.

The place is called "Bir Hooker"—Hooker's
cistern—on the maps, and so it ought to be.
The soda enterprise is due to Mr Hooker, a
scientific expert of eminent qualifications, who
had to wait many years before he induced the
Egyptian Government to take it up and make
money.   It is true the Wady has been worked
since nobody knows when; but only since the
English came has it been worked with method.
You must know that Wady Natrun is soaked
through and through with salt and soda; you
cannot walk without sliding on them, crushing

them, tasting them, breathing them. The
water of the lakes soaks through from the
Nile, thirty miles away, and takes time to
do it; the lakes begin to rise three months
after the river. The astonishing thing is that
the well water is sweet—slightly brackish to
my taste, but sweet by the standard of the
desert — while the lake water is, in places,
the colour of Condy's fluid, and a great deal
more impossible to drink. Presumably, there
are layers of impermeable clay, which prevent
the Natrun water from tainting the drink.

But never mind the drink. The water of
the lakes soaks up through the impregnated
ground till they are full: then they begin
to sink again. As they sink they leave a
thick incrustation of raw soda behind them,
till at last they dry up and leave a surface
that shines in the perpetual sun like powdery
snow. This soda is dug up in lumps: some
of it is sold raw for £7 a-ton, but the market
for this is small; the rest has to be treated.
In the sheds down by the lake, half a mile
from the station, stands all the machinery—

great solid masses of iron and steel complexity, painfully carted out here into the
lonely desert. There is the engine, neatly
tarpaulined to keep out drifting sand; there
is the crusher which crumbles up the rough
whitey-brown lumps into powder, and under
it the chamber which receives the crushings—
treble doored, for when it is working you can
hardly stand in the shed for pungent, pene-
trating dust. Then it is carried away by a
little Decauville tramway to the big red iron
vats with the two turret - shaped furnace
chimneys; then melted and run out into the
cooling vats. Then it is brought back to the
engine's sphere of influence, and whirled round
in centrifugal driers. Then it is soda, and it
fetches £4 a-ton.

All this whirling, clanking modernity, mark
you, in the empty, thirsty desert, where a
day before it had been a case for speculation
how many of our men and beasts would hold
out till we got to food, and water. The
grudging desert denies man the necessities
of life; but here was indomitable man com-

pelling it to give him luxuries out of its
very body. It was good to think this mar-
vel had been wrought by Englishmen. Only
—alas!—the engine and the furnace and the
coolers are not running now, and when next
they start they will run for Swiss.

It is all the fault of the dragging poverty
of the Egyptian Government, bound hand
and foot by Europe, not able to spend its
own money for its own good. The enterprise brought the Government a revenue, but
it could not afford the money to exploit the
soda thoroughly. For that a railway was
wanted, more plant, more buildings — in a
word, more money. So the concern has been
made over to a Swiss syndicate for fifty years.
They are building a railway, and quarrying
stone for buildings, and preparing to double,
and treble, and quadruple the machinery, and
make it pay—and fill it with Swiss. The old
story, you see: no British capital for British
Egypt!

However, it's no use crying. They can
have the soda, and we will try a little

whisky and dinner and a yarn. Next morning the glorious sun is gilding the lakes and the huts and the little bit of garden where the ox is turning up water for the sun-flowers and English vegetables, and clover for the beasts. Buy what we want for the day at the shop—for there is even a store, so permanent is the invasion of civilisation —and then on with our traps to the bullock-cart, and away. A long two miles' pull up a loose rise is a hard beginning for the oxen, since the cart is a heavy lorry, with tyres nearly a foot wide to keep on the surface of the sand. Then we are over the brow: the friendly green and mud-colour of Bir Hooker sinks behind us, and we are in the desert again.

But once more a very different desert from that we first knew. We are now on a broad track marked by wheels and ox-hoofs, horse and mule and donkey and camel tracks, and the prints of booted as well as naked feet. We are in a Regent Street of the desert. Presently we pass by a little white tower

with a sign-post: it tells how far we have
come, and how far is yet to go. This is
fatherly care, indeed. We meet men every
hour — one walking behind a camel and a
mule with an axe over his shoulder, doubtless going to work at Bir Hooker; one
driving a mule-cart; one walking all alone;
a couple of coastguards with half-a-dozen
camels. The Libyan desert seems a funny
place to meet a coastguard; but it is the
western shore of Egypt, as the Mediterranean
is the northern, and smugglers run forbidden
hasheesh from Tripoli.

Over ridges and ridges the bullock-cart
rumbles and crawls, till about two, when the
sun is very hot and drowsy, there appears a
little brown match-board on the farthest horizon. It is still an hour and a half away; but
when we get to it we find a rest-house, an
outpost of civilising Bir Hooker — a couple
of real beds, a table, a couple of chairs—in
brief, rooms, fire, light, and attendance. Four
hours' rest is due to the bullocks, and a
little rest is due to us; then, in the broad

moonlight, we must be off again. With each hour fresh invaders of civilisation appear. Here are the white, long-shadowed tents of railway surveyors. Now we are not an hour from Bir Hooker's second rest-house, which shakes hands with the railway to Cairo. And now the southward horizon seems suddenly to have become even and hard — a long, straight bar of shadow keeping pace with us. It is surely too regular, too unswerving, too set with purpose for the desert; it can only be the embankment of the coming railway. That black, dead-straight, dead-level line is the yoke for the neck of the desert. The tameless desert is tamed; from henceforth it must bow itself to bear burdens.

XIV.

THE SUDAN AND THE FELLAH.

PREPARATIONS FOR WAR—THE VALUE OF THE SUDAN—THE
POSSIBILITIES OF THE UPPER NILE—SUGAR-FACTORIES—
PROSPERITY OF THE FELLAH—HIS INCORRIGIBLE IMPROVI-
DENCE.

January 9.—War! When I left Cairo for
the desert the place was full of rumours of it
—had been for three weeks. When I got
back it was full of facts. The Lincolns gone,
the Warwicks going through from Alexandria
to-day, the Camerons to be off as soon as they
can be relieved. It's special train for Atkins
to-day, and you can see it in every street.
The gunners from the Citadel walk the streets
with the air of men whose merits are recognised
at last, and the Cameron Highlanders hail their
midnight donkeys for Kasr-el-Nil barracks in

a more richly patriotic Cameron-Highland than ever; at its best it is a great deal harder to understand than Arabic. Everybody rejoices except war correspondents, who are not invited. Now the British regiments are going up they can hardly come back without finishing the tedious job at last, and before 1899 the Khalifa will have been smashed at Omdurman, and Egypt, after half a generation of frontier war, will be at rest.

Whose fault it was that last year's advance stopped short at the Atbara, not knowing, I would rather not say. Perhaps Mr Gladstone's. But the effect of it was that Egypt was left militarily in the most exposed position imaginable. Its outposts are over thirteen hundred miles by the directest line of communication from its ultimate base, which is the Mediterranean. The Nile is falling below the possibilities of navigation, and the railhead, at this moment, is some twenty-five miles beyond Abu Hamed, and still about four times that distance short of Berber. The whole line of the Nile from Dongola to Abu

Hamed is open to attacks across the desert from Metemmeh and Omdurman.

Whether the reports of an intended dervish attack be well founded or not, it is fairly plain that the Egyptian Army, whose fighting power is still to some extent indeterminate, ought not to be left unsupported in such a position. Only unluckily this is almost the worst season of the year to support it. No river and no rail—and all the needful camels would run into money, and though the Egyptian Government hopes for a grant in aid, Sudan campaigns have to be done on the cheap. So that it seems likely that the advance will go slow for the present, creeping forward with the railway, and waiting till it is met by the rising Nile. But quick or slow, it ought to be finished this year, that Egypt may have rest.

January 10.—I have been making some inquiries about the probable effect of the reconquest on the prosperity of Egypt. The sum of them is, roughly, that for many years to come Egypt would be better off, materially,

without it. I had believed the Egyptian
Sudan a land sticky with gum and india-
rubber, and so perhaps it is. But, to begin
with, there is one thing it lacks—and that is
Sudanese. From Wady Halfa to Khartoum
the Nile banks have been depopulated. Raiding dervishes cut the men and women into
pieces, and throw the children into the Nile.
Tribes which refuse the authority of Khalifa
Abdullahi are exterminated out of hand. It
will probably be a couple of generations before
these provinces can recover enough to be a
financial strength to Egypt. In the meantime
they may pay for a very simple rough-and-
ready administration; but that will be about
all. Nothing certainly towards the cost of
their recovery. The truth is that, though
some of the Sudan provinces used to pay their
way, the Sudan as a whole was never a
pecuniary advantage to Egypt. In the old
days it used to export few commodities —
ivory, slaves, gum, and a certain brand of
dates much prized in Constantinople. Ivory
is all but exhausted now, and in any case the

hunting and transport of it rested on slave-labour : slaves, of course, are legal merchandise in Egypt no more.   The dates went straight out of the country unhandled; the gum employed some two hundred people to sort it into sizes.   The wage-bill of these two hundred is about the only direct financial return that Egypt may expect for the money she is squeezing out and bonding and pouring into the Sudan.

Political economists tell us that exports buy imports—in other words, that you cannot buy things without money, and you cannot get money without money's worth.   That being so, the prospects of an immediately lucrative British trade with the Sudan are none too sunny.   Manchester does not give away cotton - cloth for nothing; gum and india-rubber need men to get them, and the market for ostrich feathers is not limitless.   Still, there are compensations.   On the depopulated Nile banks, and on the large islands in mid-stream, have grown up dense forests.   Egypt is practically a treeless country, but for palms

and acacias : what timber there is, is pretty
well used up for water-wheels. What is
wanted for doors and windows — the Arab
does not use glass—and for railway-sleepers
comes in mostly from Syria. The afforesta-
tion of the Nile banks, if the trees are properly
husbanded, would supply a great part of this
demand from Egypt, and it is possible that
the heavily - burdened Sir William Garstin
may soon find himself charged with a Department of Forestry, in addition to his other
diversions. Another good point is the growth
of india-rubber. The rubber forests of the
Congo State and South America, vast as they
are, must give out in time, under the present
practice of felling the trees instead of tapping
them. Here, again, under proper husbandry,
will be a chance for the Upper Nile.

Passing down to Upper Egypt — that is,
the Nile-strip between Assouan and the Delta
—its possibilities in respect of sugar-growing
are prodigious. Two of the largest factories
in the world are already equipped here. I
met a gentleman to - day who lately took

shares in a company for irrigating sugar land
and crushing the canes on commission for the
native growers; after one year's work the
shares have risen from £20 to £26.   In
1896-97 the value of Egypt's sugar export
went up from £485,080 to £784,792.   If only
the reservoir at Assouan came into being, the
land on which sugar could be grown might
probably be increased fivefold.   Only, when
you hear of sugar being grown, you must not
assume too readily that it is being grown to
pay under commercial conditions.   The biggest paying sugar-workings are stale affairs,
belonging to the Daira Sainich estates.   So
that they do not have to pay rent for their
land, which, in a country where rents are so
high as they are here, makes a huge difference
in their balance-sheets.   For the rest, the
ruinously low price of sugar, here as elsewhere, is a tremendous handicap on the
young industry.   When we give preferential
treatment to the West Indies, we might
wisely give it to Egypt also.

Still, even as things now stand, the agri-
cultural prosperity of Egypt is high.   Even
with the bad cotton prices the increased area
of cultivation keeps Egypt's income steady on
this account.   Prices may go down as much
as 50 per cent, but if the cotton-bearing land
has been increased by 100 per cent, Egypt is
still the gainer.

So that, despite the Sudan campaign and
the general tightness, the fellah ought to be
prospering.   So he is ; but not as much as he
should.   The fellah is still in debt ; he always
has been in debt, and until he changes his
nature he always will be.   His taxes are
high, certainly.   I remember my Arabic
editor told me the land tax ran in places to
40 per cent.   On the average the land tax of
Egypt, which brings in half the revenue, works
out at £1 per *feddan*, which is about an acre.
As land lets easily at £5 and £6 a *feddan*,
this is only 20 per cent or less—a heavy tax,
assuredly : only a landlord who can pay £1
an acre taxes and receive £4 or £5 balance

of rent would hardly change places with some I know in England.   It is admitted, however, by the Ministry of Finance that this tax is very arbitrarily imposed—which, they say, is a thing which must be taken in hand.   The sooner, I should say, the better.

But taxes may be relaxed or remitted, as the Government will; the fellah remains in debt.   It is his nature.   The Greek, or Jewish, or Armenian usurer lives in his village; at seed-time the fellah goes to him, and borrows a little money for seeds, at 20 or 30, or even 50 per cent.   Then he borrows a little more for a new spade, and a little more to buy a donkey.   The security is the crop.   If there is a satisfactory Nile and a good harvest, the fellah is in a position to pay the usurer off, which he does—all but a little : he would not feel comfortable if he were quite free of debt.   Perhaps it has been a really good year; then he buys wood to make doors and windows for his house, he buys a cheap French bedstead instead of his mud-bank, and smokes more cigarettes than before. These are his luxuries; and the Customs returns in these articles of import show a steady rise in the fellah's standard of comfort. Even then, perhaps, he still has a fair sum in hand; but does he lay it by against next seed-time? Not he! He marries a new wife, and gives what he calls a "fantasia"— a great feast to all his friends and neighbours, with music and dancing, and joyously blues it all. Next seed-time it suddenly occurs to him that he wants seed; he goes back to the usurer and borrows for it at 20, and 30, and 50.

Then why not give the fellah a decent bank, you ask? It is easy to ask, but not so easy to do. The usurer lives in the village, and knows the circumstances, abilities, characters, of every one of his clients. He knows exactly; he lives by knowing. Could the Government put such an agent into every village to do the same? The complexity, and the expense, and the multiplication of small officials would be endless.

Or suppose private banking firms were found to go into the business : they would hardly do so without getting an assurance from the Government that their debts should rank first for recovery after taxes, and the Government would be placed in the position of collecting for the money-lender — a horrible thing to contemplate.

It is possible that private enterprise may some day do something to fill its own pockets, while helping to save the fellah from his own improvidence. In the meantime, the Egyptian Treasury has done one piece of good work by going into the usury business in competition with the usurers. Into one district, where the Greeks and Armenians were peculiarly extortionate, it sent an official with £10,000 in cash, and lent it to the fellahin at 6 per cent. They borrowed gladly and repaid punctually, but that was not all. The money-lenders, not of that district only but for many miles around, took fright. If the Government is to bring round pounds at 6 per cent, reasoned they, our occupation's gone. Down went the rate of interest all round.

But the fellah continues to borrow from them when he is short; and when he is flush he marries more wives and gives fantasias.

Arab women and children.

XV.

ALEXANDRIA.

A BUSINESS TOWN—THE WHARVES—THE ONION MARKET—QUEEN
CITY OF THE LEVANT—STATISTICS OF COMMERCE—ARAB
LABOUR AT THE DOCKS—NECESSITY FOR AN EXTENDED
HARBOUR.

January 11.—Dang, deng, ding, dong; deng,
dang, dong, ding; boom, boom, boom, boom,
boom, boom. Where on earth was I? I
thought for a moment I must be home in
Russell Square: it was just the tone of the
chimes; but I do not keep myself inside
mosquito - curtains in Russell Square. Of
course, yes; I was in Alexandria. And it
was not at all unnatural, really, to hear Christian chimes in Alexandria, nor yet to hear
any sound, or voice, or language that the earth
knows. In Alexandria nothing is foreign.

Alexandria, in brief, is a business town, and everything and everybody that can bring business or do business is in place there. And because it has its business to do, and does it, I own freely that I like the look of it better than the look of Cairo. How I shall like it to-morrow and the next day, and how I should like a month of it, having no particular business to do, is another matter; they say that to the stranger Alexandria can be dull. But, at any rate, it is not so obviously got-up for show as Cairo : it has no sights, no guides, no bogus Bedawin ; and its supply of donkey-boys is roughly proportionate to the demand. Not that Alexandria is all wharves and warehouses — by no means. It has one square which, for space and scope and order, is far superior to anything I saw in Cairo—a great oblong, acacias and palms in the middle, the Bourse at one end, law courts, banks, Cook's agency—in Egypt it is a kind of Government office without red tape—a theatre, the English church, and a statue of Mehemet Ali. It is not oriental—it doesn't affect to be; but it looks far more like a capital than anything in Cairo.

The normal street of Alexandria is less imposing. It is paved with broad square flagstones laid lozengewise : the commercial community laid them down by a self-imposed tax on each bale of cotton, and then handed them over to the municipality with a balance. Along the flags, as a rule, runs an electric tramway or a row of staples ready for one. The street is narrow ; the houses, with their embroidery of iron balcony and green shutter, are narrow-fronted and high, so that the vista down the thoroughfare is always a short one. The shops are low and cramped, but there are storeys of flats above, and rents, if nothing else, are high. And all down its length, in the full-bodied sunshine, the street is gilt with the names of the Italian and Greek retailers. Every shop, of course, with its own name, and often without its keeper's : not prosy "J. Smith, Chemist," but "Pharmacie Hippocrate," "Cornucopia, Grocery," "Ceres Corn-chandlery," "Reliance Ironmongery." Whether it is that the Levantine tradesman dislikes his name to be made too public, or that the Levantine mind generally puts all its endowment of poetry into business, I know not; but every little shop has its sign, as if they were all so many taverns.

This is only the rank and file of Alexandria's business; to see its dignity you must go down to the port. Here are wharves and wharves standing high, with the brown, tight-pressed, hoop-bound bales that stand for cotton. Here are the ships of all nations — tall British, French, Austrian, Italian, Norwegian steamers moored to the quays; a feathery cluster of spars and tackle lying out in the harbour, with the red and the crescent of Turkey, the blue and the cross of Greece; beyond them, yet again, the black hulls and pea-soup-colour upper-works of British and Russian warships. The assembly of merchantmen tells its own tale; but if you want more, come to the Onion Market and see the merchants. It is one of the subsidiary blessings of British rule, by the way, that, whereas onions used to be a rare

M

imported delicacy in Egypt, they are now exported to the tune of something like £150,000 a - year. But what was once the onion market is now the Rialto of Alexandria.

It is nearly the hour of lunch — which takes three hours, of course, according to the religious custom of the Levant; you can tell the time by the long file of rackety victorias drawn up outside. But the inside is still all bustle and buzz. It is an oblong court, open to the blue, with an arcade round it, and offices round the arcade. These offices are furnished with stools, and tables, and pigeon-holes, and especially with samples of cotton. Arab porters are carrying samples of cotton from every corner to every other corner. And in every corner, and all the sides of the arcade, and all the middle, are the merchants. Now you see what a cosmopolis is Alexandria. The English you can tell — it is not national vanity — by their clean, fresh faces, and clean, upstanding figures; the Italians mostly use square bowlers and grey double-breasted jackets; the French are usually adorned with the Legion of Honour; the Germans — well, they look like Germans, and say what we will about them, we have to respect them. But that is not half of the show. Gabbling Greeks, flashy - eyed Jews, Turks, and outright Arabs, in blue gowns, and red tarbushes, and rainbow turbans, Copts, and Syrians, and Armenians, and dwellers out of Mesopotamia, all babbling and Babelling in their own and everybody else's mother - tongue, buying cotton, selling grain, swapping sugar for coal, buying, and selling, and bartering the wealth of Egypt. Cairo may sneer at Alexandria if it will; but certainly Alexandria is a town. It is a centre, an influence, something that makes and unmakes millions. If it were American they would call it the Queen City of the Levant.

January 12. — I have got some figures about it. I don't know whether they will convey more to you than they do to me;

but they say you can prove anything by statistics, and I propose to prove the importance of Alexandria, and especially the magnificence of Great Britain. They are the 1896 figures taken from the annual table compiled by Messrs R. J. Moss & Co.; that for 1897 is naturally not ready yet.

The net register tonnage of merchant steamers cleared from Alexandria was 938,689 tons; of that 799,540 was British. Of cotton, 658,085 bales went out of Egypt—all from Alexandria, and 371,835 of them to the United Kingdom — besides 364,027 tons of cotton-seed. Of coal, 643,190 tons came to Alexandria and 966,663 to Port Said. In 1882 Alexandria took only 266,178 tons and Port Said 456,400 : if that is not quite a fair comparison, because of the troubles that year, 1884 showed 360,099 and 726,000 respectively. All this coal is from Britain, of course. The whole Customs' valuation of the year's exports tot up to 13,232,000 Egyptian pounds—an Egyptian pound is £1, 0s. 6¼d. sterling — and of that £E6,973,000 went to

Britain. The imports were £E9,829,000—of that £E3,056,000 from Britain.

We might improve on this last figure; but still we may be pretty well satisfied with the record. And so may Alexandria. It happened that a long-forgotten article by me on Port Said came into the club to-day, and the leading British merchant did me the embarrassing honour of reading it at my elbow. When he saw what I said about Port Said's claim that it ought to be the port of Egypt, he smiled. He was quite ready, of course, being an English merchant and a man of unquenched enterprise, to move himself and his family, and his dogs, and his business to Port Said, if necessary; but he does not expect to have to do it. Alexandria, he explained, is bound to keep ahead of Port Said — partly because the Government has sunk so much money in its harbour and public buildings, partly because there is no land anywhere near Port Said on which it can grow its daily beef and potatoes. So Alexandria is quite confident of its future.

Add to this that it is the cheapest port
in the world. The loading of ships is all
done by hand, or, rather, by head-and-basket,
like the coaling at Port Said. A good, but
not an unheard of, performance by this
method was lately 1600 tons of cotton-seed
in eight hours — and you wonder why we
barbarians use such clumsy, antiquated devices as cranes and donkey-engines when it
is always possible to hire the human head.
The head is cheap, too; you can load cotton-
seed at 2½d. a-ton, coal at 3d. a-ton, bale
cotton at 4d. a-ton. No docker's tanner in
Alexandria—and yet the Arab docker grins,
and pockets his piastre, and works eleven
hours and overtime, and grins again. The
human head needs Arab shoulders underneath it, and an Arab stomach underneath
that.

To wind up, Alexandria has only one
grievance, and you will allow that it is a
healthy one. Its port is far too small for
it. The port is, roughly, of the shape of a
pear—not a William, but one of the blunter

cooking sort. The south side of this is the foreshore; the north is formed by the elbow of Ras-el-Tin promontory, and a long, very obtuse-angled mole; the entrance is at the west, by the stalk of the pear, where what they call the coal-mole runs northward towards the obtuse-angled mole, which latter greatly overlaps it. The fault is that all the northern part of the harbour, under the obtuse angle, is too shoal to be of much use, while there is eight and nine fathoms water outside the port west of the coal-mole. What Alexandria wants is a new mole, roughly opposite the end of the northern mole, to take in two hundred acres of this space, adding it to the harbour, which would then be more of the shape of a William, and less of a cooking pear. Then new jetties could be built from the present coal-mole, and there would be new berths for at least a dozen ships.

Alexandria, so far as I could take its opinion, does not suggest where the money is to come from. But it pays stiff Customs

and stiff port dues, and it has a right to
say what it wants. And, for my part,
having conceived in two days a great respect for Alexandria's enterprise and industry, I hope that when the Sudan is reconquered, and the reservoir is made, and the
Caisse de la Dette and the mixed tribunals
abolished, and the taxes reduced — I hope
that Alexandria will get it.

XVI.

LORD CROMER AND HIS WORK.

VELVET AND STEEL—A MAN WHO KNOWS HIS OWN MIND—A
DIPLOMATIC TRIUMPH—WHEN IS ENGLAND GOING TO LEAVE
EGYPT?—THE ATTITUDE OF FRANCE—THE FRENCH ABROAD
—NATIVE VIEWS OF THE ENGLISH OCCUPATION—A FRENCH
EDITOR'S OPINION — OUR ONE FAILURE — ENGLAND OR
TURKEY.

January 13.—To read Egyptian-French ac-
counts of Lord Cromer, you would picture him
a stiff-browed, hard-mouthed, cynical, taciturn
martinet. To look at the real man, you would
say that he gave half his time to sleep, and
the other half to laughing. Lolling in his
carriage through the streets of Cairo, or
lighting a fresh cigarette in his office, dressed
in a loose-fitting grey tweed and a striped
shirt, with ruddy face, short white hair, and
short white moustache, with gold - rimmed

eye-glasses half-hiding eyes half-closed, mellow of voice, and fluent of speech,—is this the perfidious Baring, you ask yourself, whom Frenchmen detest and strive to imitate? this the terrible Lord Cromer whom Khedives obey and tremble? His demeanour is genial and courteous. His talk is easy, open, shrewd, humorous. His subordinates admire, respect, even love him. He is the mildest - mannered man that ever sacked Prime Minister. Only somehow you still feel the steel stiffening the velvet. He is genial, but he would be a bold man who would take a liberty with him : he talks, only not for publication ; he is loved, yet he must also be obeyed. Velvet as long as he can, steel as soon as he must—that is Lord Cromer.

He has had the hardest row to hoe of any British representative abroad in our generation, and out of it he has raised the best crop. Few men have ever had to face so much opposition : few have so triumphantly parried and quelled it. He has stood for

years in the van of British diplomatic battle;
yet the shock of it has never moved, never so
much as ruffled, him. Time upon time the
strongest coalitions have been formed against
him; the Khedive, the Cabinet, France,
Russia, Turkey have combined to humiliate
him. At his back he has had England, only
often an England that did not know her
mind. But his own mind Lord Cromer has
always known, and when things went too far
his opponents came to know it too.

At one time it was the recognised rule of
Egyptian Prime Ministers—when in doubt
attack Lord Cromer. They don't do it now.
At one time it was the favourite diversion of
the Khedive; he is not so fond of it now.
At one time France was never weary of it;
she lets him alone now. They have mistaken
accidents for essentials, things that did not
matter for things that did; Lord Cromer has
not. They have lost their tempers, and he has
not. They have failed in their resolution;
he has not. Often he has appeared beaten
on single points and for the time; on the

main issue and in the end he has beaten them all. And at present, thanks to Lord Cromer, there is no Egyptian question.

The Egyptian question has been answered. Lord Cromer has sat still, declining to be worried or flurried, until it has answered itself. The question was, When is England going to quit Egypt? The right answer was, Never. The provisional answer given from time to time has been, When, first, it is quite certain that no other Power will enter Egypt; and, second, Egypt is capable of setting up a tolerable Government for itself. In the course of the past fifteen years the latter answer to the question has gradually approximated to the former. "When" has come gradually nearer and nearer to "Never."

Twice in these times we have voluntarily entered upon negotiations with a view to withdrawal; each time France has petulantly frustrated them. We need not be surprised at France's irritation. If we in 1882 had incomparably the greater interest in Egyptian trade, it must be owned that France had done

more for the country. France gave Egypt
the Canal—perhaps a doubtful blessing from
the native point of view; she commenced
giving her the Barrage; she gave her the
law. French manners, habits, ideas had
spread far more deeply into the social daily
life of the country than ours—more deeply
than any European influence except Italian.
The French language was more generally
known; it was even the official language of
the country, and in theory is still. But if,
having done so much, France drew back at
the critical moment and declined to. risk her
skin to save her work, it is with herself she
should be angry, not with us.

But France has sulked, and because she
has sulked her policy in Egypt has been a
string of blunders. She locks up Egypt's
money in the Caisse de la Dette : well, then,
it will only take us the longer to put the
country in order. She refuses funds for the
reconquest of the Sudan : well, then, Britain
advances it, and is it likely Britain will let
go of territories conquered with her own

money? She refuses funds for the Nile Reservoir : [1] well, we are certainly not going to leave Egypt without it. She refuses to modify the Capitulations, or even to give up her separate post-office : well, is a country that is unfit to manage its own post by itself fit to manage anything?

Every French move has defeated itself, and it looks lately as if France had at last discovered this. She has made no difficulty about advances from the Caisse reserve for irrigation; about the present Sudan expedition she has not yet uttered one word. There are those who trace this saner mood from the date of Sir Michael Hicks-Beach's flat declaration that we are not to be worried out of

[1] *February 24.*—To Wady Halfa, where I read this over, too late to correct what I wrote about it in the chapter on Irrigation, comes a flimsy bit of paper from Reuter & Co., to the effect that the contract for the Reservoir is actually signed. It is to take the form of a couple of barrages at Assuan and Assiut respectively. But who is going to pay for these, and how, and when, the flimsy does not say. Still, I do not apologise. If the French and Russian commissioners on the Caisse de la Dette have released the money, it confirms what I say just below. If they have not, it justifies what I say just below.

Egypt; perhaps they are right. At any rate, Sir Michael said well; we are not to be worried out—and France has left off worrying.

There is also another reason for not taking France too seriously in Egypt. Frenchmen cannot stand the climate. I do not speak so much physically as spiritually: hardly a Frenchman ever can stand any climate but that of France. Now meet an Englishman of sixty who has not spent five years at home since he was seventeen; he grumbles, of course, but as long as he can do his work he is game to stay a year or two more. For that matter there is an old gentleman in Lower Egypt who has been in the country sixty years, and has so far acclimatised himself as to marry three native wives, each with money. But take a Frenchman of forty in a public service and offer him a pension; he is away to France at once. He is able, honest, and patriotic; he knows he is doing good work for himself, for Egypt, and, indirectly, for France; the climate is less severe for a Frenchman than for an Englishman,

the mode of life is far more congenial, the
salary, relatively to home standards, far more
princely.   But give him a chance to go back
to France, and he throws up work and salar
together, and is off to spend his pension in
his native *café*.   That is why France, for
all her brilliant imagination and courage and
cleverness, has never made a great colony,
and never will.

And now what about the natives?   Well,
there is a party against us, as you know;
and as the Khedive is the leader of it, it
is perhaps just worth mentioning.   But hardly
more, for any danger there is in it.   Like
France, it is troublesome as long as we let
it trouble us: when we don't, it sinks at
once into silence—or as near silence as an
Egyptian can attain.   Take an illustration.
Last summer, I think it was, the inhabitants of a certain village in Lower Egypt
took occasion of Lord Cromer's absence on
leave to stone a company of mounted infantry which was marching through.   Where-
upon Mr Rennell Rodd, who was in charge,

arose and had the village — naturally with the consent of the Egyptian authorities — surrounded by that same company of mounted infantry, while the ringleaders were arrested ; and these are now unloading rails and sleepers at Wady Halfa, which they dislike. Soon afterwards the 21st Lancers were marched from Cairo to Suez. Barrels of beer were provided by a grateful fellahin as they passed by, and everywhere they were received with tumultuous joy and affection. It only needs a little firmness.

But what, meanwhile—merely as a matter of curiosity, if you like—do they say to our continued occupation and administration of their country? If you ask them they will readily answer that it is very wrong. "Certainly you should leave Egypt," they say ; "it is not your country, and you ought not to keep it." Just the same with officials. It is a great grievance that there are too many English officials ; but go to a grumbler and say to him that you are appointing a native inspector of irrigation or a native judge

N

in his district. "Excellent!" he will say. "It is an excellent thing to employ native officials; only would you mind sending him to some other district? My water and my justice I would sooner have from an Englishman." So they are almost unanimous that we ought to go; only when it comes to the point of when and how, there begin to be difficulties. Nubar Pasha is quite certain he could govern the country beautifully, if only the English officials would all go away and leave him the Army of Occupation. Tigrane Pasha is absolutely confident of his ability to govern the country, if only the Army of Occupation would go away and leave him the officers and irrigation engineers. Observe that both these gentlemen, honest and capable as they are, are Armenians—that is to say, no more Egyptians than Lord Cromer is, and without Lord Cromer's habit and tradition of rule. How long would they remain there? As for the editor of the principal French paper of Egypt, he is a great deal sharper-sighted. "Certainly you ought

to go," says he; "as I say, your action here
is an abomination" — he does say so, too —
"but as for me, I go also by the last boat
before you do."

And that is what would happen. The wise
virgins would leave by the last boat before
us, with their realised property; the foolish
ones would leave by the first boat after,
without it. We have done much for the
Egyptian; we have given him security, justice, water, better times than he has ever
had before. We have even gone far to make
a soldier of him. Our record is one which
any other nation would be proud of, which
no other nation could achieve. But one
thing, so far, we have failed with — the
Egyptian. We have not made a man of
him. Take the very best of them — an intelligent, industrious, honest official, whom
his English chief is sincerely trying to push
forward into a commanding position. He
will come to that chief, and beg and pray
to be relieved of responsibility. He doesn't
like it. It terrifies him. He is not a man.

There are only two forces in Egypt to-day. Of the two forces, one you know—Lord Cromer, Sir William Garstin, who gives water, and Sir John Scott, who gives justice, and the screw-guns on the Citadel, which can shell any street in Cairo at the call of a telephone. The other force you may see on one side in the gabbling fanaticism of El Azhar Mosque, on the other in the Turkish aristocracy. If we go, the Turk must rule again. The Turk is a gentleman, and a man, and a ruler of men. Only he would rule the Arab in his own way — the old way. The water would all go to his fields; the cases would all go in his favour; the labour would all go, unpaid, to build his palace; his rent and his taxes would be thrashed out of the Arab with a stick. And then—since the Arab is by now accustomed to other things—another Arabi.

Therefore, we shall go on ruling in our way.

XVII.

BITS OF OLD AND NEW.

RUMOURS OF WAR—THE PYRAMIDS—THE VIEW FROM THE GREAT
PYRAMID—A VISIT TO THE ARSENAL.

January 28. — I thought I was leaving
Egypt, not for good—one does not like the
idea of never seeing Egypt again—but at
any rate for a good while. Now here I am
back again in a fortnight. And if the air
breathed war when I went away, it breathes
fire and slaughter now. The Government,
you must know, in pursuance of that policy
which has always drawn a mysterious and
perhaps prudent veil over its intentions about
the Sudan, has decided that correspondents
are not to be allowed to go to Berber, which
is a little behind the actual front. There
are fifteen thousand men or so beyond Mail-

head, so that it can hardly be want of transport that prompts the decision; besides which, correspondents always find their own transport. Moreover, there were half-a-dozen correspondents at Berber last year, who did the place no harm I ever heard of · moreover, there is a censor.

All this is of more interest to me than it is to you, perhaps. But I am moved to reflect on it by the fact that, thanks to the Government's obscurantism, all Cairo at this moment is rustling with the wildest rumours. There has been a defeat at the front with heavy loss; the gunboats are partly stranded and partly captured; Slatin Pasha — *O malheureux*, remarks a French organ with feeling — has been retaken by the dervishes.[1] As for the Egyptian army, the gloomiest reports go abroad concerning it. The Egyptians, they say, have been harried to mutiny over the railway; the Sudanese deprived of their women till they mutiny, too; you

[1] *February 18.*—Need I say that the first person I saw at Wady Halfa was Slatin?

would think half the army was shot away for insubordination by this time. Of course all these stories are the wildest nonsense: that is declared sufficiently by the stamp of the people that circulate them. But the fact remains that Cairo is very uneasy. It doesn't matter much, to be sure; but so far as it does matter, the Government is to blame for acting as if it had things to conceal.

January 29.—To relax my mind—for you can't show yourself in hotel or restaurant or street without being told or asked for some new thing—I have been taking a morning with the Pyramids. There is no fretful rumour - mongering about them. They have looked down quite apathetically on more great things than you or I or any history-book ever heard of, and they are not going to trouble themselves now about the movements of dervishes or anybody else. It was a great refreshment to go out and look at them—so enormous, so moveless, so battered by time and spoilers, and yet so imperturbably indestructible.

Most people are disappointed with them; they say they are not near so large as they expected. I don't know what these people looked for; they are quite large enough for me. You must know that they stand quite alone in the desert—a village or two and a hotel in sight of them; but this environment is part of them, not they part of it. They are not a part of anything, the Pyramids: they just stand up, themselves, dominating the flat Egyptian fields on one side, and the furrows of the desert on the other. Large or not, they get all the advantage of their size, whatever it is; and, in truth, their size is sufficient for any purpose. There is something in the shape of a pyramid, too, that makes it an impressive monument—it stands so solidly upon its feet, so square and immovable; yet the taper of it prevents it from ever looking unwieldy. The third pyramid is small—not in itself, but by comparison— and if I had been the king that built it, I would rather have been forgotten altogether than only remembered as the man who put

up a pyramid insignificantly smaller than
those of his predecessors. But the other
two — they must be surely the sublimest
monuments in the world. No others can
give so crushing an impression of absolute
independence of everything — of stability
equal to looking down on every convulsion
and cataclysm that the world can know,
and still stably looking down on what shall
follow on the end of it.

Of course I walked up the Great Pyramid.
I am afraid there is nothing particularly ex-
citing about it. It is rather like walking up
a small mountain. You have your guides—
you need not, unless you want to, but it
saves a lot of trouble—and they take you
firmly by each hand and pull at you. The
slope of the Pyramid is in steps—here even
like a staircase, there broken away like a
cliff-face—and the only difficulty is that you
often have to cock your leg as high as your
head to get from one to the other. And
when you get up there is a small flat space
to stand on while you look at Cairo and

Egypt and the desert. Only, to tell the truth, Cairo and Egypt and the desert look exactly as you knew they would look. A jumble of brown buildings for Cairo, with the minarets of the Citadel mosque shooting up above it; a chess-board of green and brown for Egypt; a boundless sea of sand for the desert—that is all you see from the Great Pyramid. More of it than you can see from anywhere else; but more of just the same thing.

January 30.—To correct, in its turn, the impression of the untroubled Pyramids, I went to-day to see the Arsenal. It is on the lower slopes of the Citadel, and it is presided over by a nephew of Gordon. In England he would be a subaltern of Engineers; in Egypt he is the man who forges the weapons which are to avenge his uncle. I don't know enough about such things to describe to you the engines which are turning out Egypt's armoury; but the whole thing is typical of British Egypt. Here is the old second-hand material, the bad native workmen, and the practical, undiscouraged Englishman, who surmounts everything by his ingenuity and his perseverance. There is hardly a machine in the Arsenal that is running now on the same work as it was built for. They are all old and damaged and derelict; but they have been patched up and adapted and fitted for something or other that will tend to keep Egypt going. There is one machine cutting off the ends of Martini barrels, whose rifling has been worn away, and turning them into carbines. Here is another machine using the cut-off ends as part of the sight for a Maxim-Nordenfeldt. Here is everything in preparation that the Egyptian Army needs, from gunboats to camel-saddles and boots. All done on the cheap, with sweat and swearing—but all done. The material is Egypt, and the triumph over it is Britain: British Egypt is the picturesque incredible combination of the two.

XVIII.

THE PILGRIMS.

THE DRAGOMAN ADDRESSES THE TOURISTS—THE NOMENCLATURE
OF DONKEYS—THE TOMB OF THI—MORE ENJOYABLE TOMBS.

February 2.—The dragoman—a fat figure in
green robe and wonderful silk skirt, a fat
brown face below a gold - worked turban —
entered the dining-room, faced his flock with
proud modesty, and clapped his hands. Instantly the clatter of lunch sank to expectant
silence.

"Ladies and shentleman," he began, in the
long-drawn accents of the muezzin who sum-
mons the faithful to prayer, " in one half an
hour the steamer will stop at Bedrechein.
Then we shall take donkeys and ride three-
quarters of an hour to the gre-eat statue of
Rameses the Second. Then we shall ride

three-quarters of one hour to the gre-e-eat pyramids of Sikkara, and we shall enter the gre-e-eat tomb of Thi. Then we shall return one hour and one half to the steamer, where you shall have tea." Then he paused, and a benevolent grin slowly overspread the acreage of his face. "Ladies and shentleman," he pursued, "live together and love one another. Remember the words of the programme: Birds in deir little nestes aggree."

He was gone: almost immediately the Cook's tourist steamer Rameses the Great had pulled up at Bedrechein, and our pilgrimage had begun. There were exactly eighty of us—English, French, Germans, Belgians, South Africans, Americans, and Australians, from the uttermost ends of the earth. There were many elderly men, a great host of young women, five men under thirty, and three children under ten. Our mood was devotional. We regarded the dragoman with respect, and the great tomb of Thi with awe. Our trusty cameras were slung at our backs: our diaries lay in our cabins with our stylographs at half-cock beside them: the two hours since we left Cairo had been given to the diligent study of a book full of queer pictures of circles and hieroglyphic ducks and hares couchant, with which Mr Cook had presented each of us on leaving. And now we were about to see all these things. Up and down the long dining-tables every face was set with high purpose.

Already Mohammed was on the sandy beach, selecting donkeys. Out we streamed after him into a sea of waving brown arms and legs surging furiously over the little island of beasts. Some of the elder ladies mounted chairs, and were borne off, palanquin fashion, on the shoulders of four boatmen. The rest climbed with delicious quavers on to donkeys, the donkey-boys screamed, and yelled, and whacked, and we were off.

I fancy the donkey was one of the few animals not worshipped by the ancient Egyptians; it has its revenge now. The tomb of Thi was forgotten, and seventy minds—allowing for ten who did not face the fatigues of

the expedition—were fixed intently on donkeys. "Have you a satisfactory donkey, sir,
may I ask?" says the Chicago colonel, gravely.
"Say, Juliet, what's your donkey's name?"
"M'Kinley, the boy says." "So's mine;
they're all M'Kinleys here, I guess." It does
not occur to the American mind—which leaves
its vigilant shrewdness behind it when it
crosses the Atlantic—that the Nile donkey
has as many names as the old Nile kings.
M'Kinley and Yankee Doodle for an American rider, Jubilee for a British, Moses or
Abraham for the pious, Ta-ra-ra Boom-de-ay
for the worldling—the name of the useful
creature follows automatically the prospects
of backsheesh.

By now we had passed under a grove of
dusty palms, over the railway embankment,
threaded the mud-walled alleys of the village,
and were out, a straggling column a couple of
miles long, among fields of young clover and
springing corn. We had not waited to hear
Mohammed lecture on the great statue of
Rameses. We came on it suddenly among

palm trees; but it has tumbled down and got broken, and hieroglyphics are crawling all over it. It is not bad for a barbarian people, but not the sort of thing to detain light-minded children like Jack, and Nellie, and me. For that matter, Nellie couldn't stop if she wanted to: with her hat tilted off her freckled face, and her red hair floating behind her, she has been scolding her donkey-boy for half an hour in useless Australian. "Stop, you horrid boy, when I tell you! Oh, you are nasty! Oh, do tell him to stop. I've told him in good English, and if he doesn't understand that I should like to know what he does understand." Whereon the half-naked Arab, conceiving himself to be earning high praise and backsheesh, falls to whacking the donkey mightily. "Yes, go quick," he pants; "very good donkey, good boy, good backsheesh." And "No!" screams Nellie, rocking helplessly to and fro. "No! Do you know what 'no' means? Well!"

But it doesn't need the concentrated indignation of that "Well!"—we are all stopping.

We have arrived at something. It doesn't look very much—a clearing in the up-and-down of sand, with a skylight and a path leading down to an underground door. Still, it must be an antiquity, and we try to compose our minds. The donkey-boys brought clover inside their shirts, and have been trying to induce us to buy their own fodder and feed their own donkeys with it, but now they see that we are about to proceed to business. "Tomb," they cry, with enthusiasm, "tomb of Mera," and smile all over, as if you wanted nothing but a good tomb to ensure a happy afternoon. "Oh, it's only a tomb, is it?" says Jack, and "Well, all I can say is," adds Nellie, "I don't think much of it." But the colonel is perturbed even unto making a short speech. "Ladies and gentlemen, I am inclined to think that we should have been better advised to have proceeded less precipitately. I guess he may have gone around to that other tomb he mentioned; then we shall have missed considerable information."

The facile "I don't care!" which springs to

Nellie's lips is choked in the general gasp of
consternation. But somebody looks back to
where the donkeys tail out across the sand
and raises a joyful cry. Here is Mohammed.
He dismounts with dignity, and orders the
doors of the tomb to be thrown open. Show
your tickets at the door, without which one
may not see antiquities. Take a candle from
the guardian at the door and step in. The
moment has come; we are in a tomb!

Except for the sheer delight and impertinence of being in the tomb of somebody else
very much older than yourself, I am not sure
there is very much in it after all. It is half-
a-dozen chambers hewn in the rock which
underlies the desert sand, and our company
quite fills it up. There are some rudimentary
carvings on the wall still splashed with faint
red and yellow, and there is a statue of the
entombed himself — an angular person of a
brick-red colour attired in what Mohammed
tactfully calls a kilt. Furthermore, Mohammed, scraping the walls with his nose and
a candle, at length discovers a hieroglyphic

which he alleges he can read.   He bellows
it out in thunderous triumph: "How many,
how many hat?" it sounds like, and the re-
verberating tomb takes up the query, "How
many, how many hat?"   "That proves it, you
see," says the maiden lady in yellow hair
and blue spectacles: "it must be the Sixth
Dynasty."

Two more enjoyable tombs we accomplished
that afternoon.   One was a cemetery for sacred
bulls, but the mummies have all been taken
away, and it did not differ materially from the
monument of a mere high priest.   However,
we were very careful to get the dynasty right
in each case, and if we had only looked into
eleven graves when there were really twelve,
we went back with a candle to look into the
twelfth.   If looking into empty holes will
enrich our minds, we have every prospect of
coming home very superior spirits to all you
who have never been up the Nile.

But now we are out of school.   "Everything seen, ladies and shentleman; you can
go home," says Mohammed, and off we go.

The air is cool now over the corn and clover; the fellah pushing at his wooden plough is thinking of going home. Some of us are wondering how stiff we shall be to-morrow, others striving to contain the name of "How many, how many hat" till we get to our diaries. Speaking for Nellie and Jack and myself, I am not sure there was not a thought of tea. Anyhow, here is the steamer again. The tour is only seven hours old, and of that five have been spent ashore, but already the steamer is home. Here are Arabs to brush the dust of Thi off our boots, and tea is waiting on deck. We are warm and thirsty: what more can anybody ask? "Were the objects interesting?" asks the old gentleman who did not go. Of an enthralling fascination, we tell him—and so they were, I don't know why: yet everybody, you find, has been enjoying it enormously. So the steamer casts off, and Jack and Nellie turn to high tea, and the other pilgrims, before dinner be ready, seize greedily upon note-books.

XIX.

THE PANORAMA.

February 5.—Breakfast 8.30, lunch 1.0, tea
4.30, dinner 7.0, lights out 11.0. "Early to
bed and early to rise," remarked Mohammed,
in one of his latest speeches, "makes you
healthy, we-ealthy, and wise." For myself,
I was healthy before, and have given up
all hope of ever being wealthy or wise, and
I could do with a later breakfast and lights
on a little longer. But that is a small
thing; and, after all, Mr Cook, though
stern, is very kind, and I am not sure but
his regulations are for the best. For the

keynote of the Nile life is peace; it is an existence placid, regular, reposeful.

There is just enough variety in it to keep your mind awake, and just enough sameness to keep it off the stretch. There is just enough excursionising ashore to persuade you that you are not lazy, and just enough lazying aboard to assure you that you are enjoying rest. You pick up letters on the way, enough to remind you that you are of the world, and to convince you blessedly that for the moment you are not in it. A vision of half-barbarous life passes before you all day, and you survey it in the intervals of French cooking. You are not to worry, not to plan, not to arrange about anything; you are just to sit easy and be happy.

You come up in the morning, and there, steel-blue in the sun, shines the benevolent Nile. You forget how many days you have been looking at it; you could look at this miracle for ever. Just now we are under a bank of low, brown cliff, the frontier of the desert. On the other side is a flat green plain — so flat that you can see no end to it, though the transparent blue film of another distant line of hills reminds you that on that side also the desert presses. Over the green rim rise groves of palms, the silhouette of a man with a mattock, of a woman striding erect beneath her water-jar, of a fat, turbaned sheikh on a donkey. Now we are swinging across from under the bluffs past an eyot of yellow sand towards the fertile side; already the navigable channel is narrow and devious, even at this season, and the long-gowned pilot on the bridge seldom has his hand off the wheel. Now the solitary palms thicken into groves with a clump or two of denser acacias : here is a village. Mud huts pierced by loop-hole windows, rush firewood stacked on the roofs, black veils carrying water, young boys, half blue shirt, half brown nakedness, paddling in the river. Rural Egypt at Kodak range — and you sitting in a long chair to look at it.

February 6.—Through all its twists and changes the Nile never loses its character of the ancient begetter of life. The bordering hills, the green clover, the mud huts, the black yashmaks, and the blue galabeahs —they are all the setting and the fruit and the children of the Nile. Steel-blue in the sunshine, his waters are coffee-brown in the shade—that is the off-scouring of the Abyssinian mountains, the Egypt - making mud. You take him in your bath of a morning; he is vestry carts to look at, but velvet to wallow in. And now we are plugging past a twenty-foot river bank, semaphored with miles of water - hoists. At the bottom a man pulls down the cross-bar till the straw-plaited bucket dips in the river; the weight at the other end of the beam pulls it up, and he empties it into a mud hollow six feet up the bank. Down dips another calabash to meet it, and lifts it to the next pool. Then down dips a third, and the fertiliser is at the top of the bank swishing away through the ditches on to the fields.

Clumsy irrigation, you say; but Egypt adds this to its other wonders, that machinery has not yet been able to supplant the human body. They have tried turbines and hydraulic rams, and all sorts of contrivances, but they do not work, or work too expensively, and they fall back on machine-saving labour again.

And with that it is lunch-time — for one glory of the Nile life is that each meal seems to follow half an hour on the last, and yet you are always hungry. At the end of lunch we shall find ourselves opposite a landing-stage, with donkeys in the background. The other day—which day was it? Thank heaven! I do not know, so you can see what a holiday this is—it was Assiout, the largest town of the Upper Egyptian Nile, the old starting-point of the forty-day desert caravans to Darfur. Backsheesh, backsheesh—the national anthem of Egypt—strikes familiarly on our ears: we are callous to it now. Also we have lost our awe of antiquities; in our leisure we talk of Egypt as it is, without bothering about the eleventh dynasty, or else of our own affairs—books and money and war, cotton in Bolton, and sulphate on the Rand, sheep in South Australia, and coal round Pittsburg. So we go out and seize on donkeys, with an easy and irresponsible mind.

We scuttle off like a specially irregular troop of irregular cavalry, kicking up a choking dust-storm. We stream out on to the main road, embanked against flood-time, and across the railways. We plunge tumultuously into the dark bazaar, and buy two-penny-halfpenny pottery and fivepenny cutting whips. Then in and out we thread the mud-walled alleys, and arrive at the bottom of what Mohammed calls the mountain: really it is only the ridge between green and desert. We patter up the crumbling shale to the tomb of Merry Christmas — that at least is what his name sounds like, and he was either a general or a high priest in something between the fifth and twenty-fifth dynasties. What does it matter? We don't come here

to learn lessons; we are children out for a
holiday. The Chicago colonel himself has
left off taking down the names of tomb-
holders in his note - book, and now uncon-
scientiously copies them into his diary out of
the guide.

Market-place, Egypt.

It is much more to the point when Mohammed throws a stone down a hole, and
the priest of the somethingth dynasty whirs
up out of it in the shape of an enormous
bat. Nelly lets out a whoop of joy and

terror, and the younger maidens wonder if
it is roosting in their hair, and the elder
maidens are led to seats on rocks. Mummies
and hieroglyphics we have grown old among,
but a real live bat is something to talk about.
Why not? A little thing—but are we not
children out of school?

Then those of us that are feeling very
well—and the proportion rises day by day—
pound on up to the very top of the rocks,
and look down. Below us in the haze basks
Assiout, with its minarets. At our very feet,
on the edge of the belt of cultivation, is
another city—a city of mud walls, and white-
wash, and domes. It seems as large as Assiout, but quite empty — only it is not, for
it is a thickly - peopled cemetery. On our
right is the valley of the Nile — a steely
thread through broad acres of glowing, living
green. This is already the second crop of
clover since the flood reached its heights in
September: three weeks back it was just
sprouting; to-day it covers the earth like a
carpet. And leftward and behind us is the

desert, the cruel, haunting, yellow desert, with camel-trains trailing over it like ants. In that one view you see all Egypt—the river, the life of the valley, and the death of the desert; the city of the living in the one, the city of the dead with its foot on the threshold of the other.

Then back to our welcoming steamer. Cast off, and then more Nile, more Egypt—daily more familiar, daily more fascinating. We are in the region of sugar-refineries now; for every minaret there rises a tall stack vomiting black smoke. One we have visited—a jangle of whirring wheels, cane sliding up whole and coming down broken shreds and oozing juice, sweltering furnaces, filters, tanks full of glutinous sweetness, and whirling centrifugal crystallisers. Toiling in this western jangle were just the same grinning, half-naked, chocolate Arabs as hoist up the water with their antediluvian levers and buckets, or go out on the merry backsheesh hunt. We anchored there for the night. On one side was the belching factory, with its three

big chimneys and ten little ones: they work
day and night during the two months of the
crushing season, and the blackness of the
smoke blotted out the falling sun.   But close
beside them was a grove of drooping palms
and a dome and minaret — black, too, but
clear black tracery against the blazing gold
of sunset.   The gold faded, and the white
moon lit to silver; the tender blue curtain
of darkness brooded down over the floating
blue Nile; the minarets suddenly dwindled
into slender columns of fire, with the hanging lanterns of Ramadan.   Close at their side
the chimneys belched and belched, griming
the moonlight.   It was yet another paradox
of Egypt—the old and the new.

XX.

THE RUINS.

LUXOR—THEBES—COLOSSAL RUINS—THE TOMBS OF THE KINGS
—KARNAK—THE COLOSSI OF MEMNON.

February 8.—Until I saw Luxor I had the poorest idea possible of the abilities and achievements of the ancient Egyptians. When I had seen it I only wished I could have been an ancient Egyptian myself to see Luxor in its prime.

For Luxor stands on the site of the great city of Uast—ancient Thebes—the fame of whose greatness had come even to Homer's ears when he sang of its hundred gates and twenty thousand war-chariots. But Homer, at the very beginning of European civilisation, was a sucking babe to Thebes. Thebes had passed her heyday and was be-

ginning to grow old before Homer was. Yet
after Homer had lived and died, and all the
great Greeks, and through the days of Alex-
ander the Great, and even after that, the
wonders of Thebes were still accumulating
from year to year. From the twenty-fifth
century before Christ down to the fourth,
Thebes was embellishing itself with fresh
wonders perpetually.

To-day it is quite deruinate, tumbled down
and knocked to pieces, scraped to powder and
stifled in sand. Yet it is so huge in its over-
throw, so grandly and yet pathetically indestructible, that you leave it dazed and
stupid. The mind will not take it all in.
If it were standing complete you might possibly grasp the plan of it for all its vastness.
As it is, the thing baffles and eludes you.
Here, you cannot but see, was one of the
greatest marvels of the world—yet you can
never know what it was like. You can see
the parts of it, but you can never, never
attain to any conception of the whole. Other
ruins never afflicted me with any sense of

loss. They are ruined, and there's an end of it : probably they look much better as they are. But the ruins of Thebes are almost tragic in their suggestion that something is lost that can never be recovered. They seem struggling to tell you some great secret, and they are doomed to dumbness for ever.

So that I cannot give you any idea of the ruins in and about Luxor: I have none for myself. I have only a string of single re-collections : you must be content if I unwind you that.

When the boat pulls up at Luxor the land-ing-stage appeared to be a colossal temple. Really this is across the road, but, even so, it was wonder enough. Arcades of huge pillars, some complete, some half broken down, some sprawling in hideous dislocation —they loomed grey and motionless and solemn in face of the ancient river and the flaming sunset. The dust and filthiness of Luxor village clustered round them and half-covered them ; the donkey-boys and beggars bawled before them ; they stood still and soundless,

P

heeding nothing of it. As we went to bed almost under them they seemed to be rebuking squalid, modern Egypt—rebuking modernity altogether, that was so small and fretting, while they remained so great and unsurprised.

February 9.—To-day it was a long canter on the other side of the river to the tombs of the old kings. The serpent of donkeys wound up a long valley, rock-cored, but half silted up with sand, and crunching with loose stones. A cluster of Arabs, blue and black in their galabeahs, and touched with the white of their turbans, showed that we had arrived. And there, in the face of the rock walls, one, two, three—a dozen and more—were little square holes of about the height of a man. They are closed in with iron gates now, for the Egyptian Government supports its monuments by selling tickets to view them; but as you go through, that is the last hint of to-day. You are going down a slope, then down a flight of broken stone steps, and it is time to light your candle. You come into a small square chamber—all hewn out of the naked

rock, but cut all over with hieroglyphics and
rude pictures of outlandish men and mon-
strous-headed gods.   You hold up your candle
to them ; here looks out the head of a hawk,
there of a cat, there of a man or woman almost
as grotesque as they.   You can still see faintly
upon them the blue and yellow and vermilion
with which they once shone—shone for no
eye to look upon.

Lower down, by more broken staircases,
blind with darkness and choked with dust,
you will come to the sleeping chamber of the
dead Pharaoh.   The bat that rushes whirring
out as you go in might be his soul, shy and
indignant that after these thousands of years
of rest his home has been broken open and
has echoed to voices.   There is his sarco-
phagus — that great hollow mass of black
granite.   The lid—it must weigh tons upon
tons of itself—is split asunder : the mummy
is gone—stolen and sold for a rich man's fad,
or taken away for schoolgirls to giggle at
in a museum.   The tomb, which was sealed
up so well that when it was opened they

found footprints thirty-three centuries old as clear printed as those of last minute, is left empty and desolate. I suppose that while there exists a demand for mummies political economy will not be satisfied without a supply. But it does seem hard upon King Seti that they have taken away his poor shrivelled body and hollow-socketed head for people to pay at the door to look at. He kept his secret so well and so long, and he was so horribly afraid lest he should be disturbed. Better if he could have rested for ever, unknown of, unrecked of, in the silent heart of his mountain.

February 10.—These things, however, are only the setting : the jewel of Luxor is Karnak. I saw it first by moonlight. Along the dim, dusty road you suddenly come on a tall pylon — a square gateway, inclining slightly towards the top, narrow for its great height. Then Karnak begins. Soon you are in an avenue of couchant sphinxes, defaced lion heads, ghostly in the white light. In front of you tower what look like two fort-

resses, two mountains of masonry. They are
so huge that you at first mistake them for
real hills ; yet they are only another gateway.
Pass that and you are in a court littered with
broken shafts and beheaded pedestals, fragments of fallen columns, and limbs of statues
as tall. On your right gleams doubtfully a
smaller temple : two huge statues guard it
at the entry : within, to right and left, stand
others, handless, headless, shivered to the
waist ; of some nothing remains but a pair
of prodigious shapeless feet thrust forward
out of nothing.

But keep along the central aisle. Now you
are in the great hall, standing like an ant
between rows on rows of giant columns
Those at the back are half hidden in rubble
that climbs to where the roof was ; the nearest stand free, and it takes ten people's arms
to encircle one of them. You stand abashed
beneath them ; wherever you look more tremendous pillars press in upon you ; the blue-
blacked, star-pierced heaven is only a little
slit far, far above you. You are almost glad

to escape from the impression of their majesty, and be out again in the moonlight you are accustomed to. Now before you rises an obelisk, a slight shaft flying up to bathe its point in the moonlight; the night is so still and clear that you can see the compasses and boats and owls that are carved on it. And beside it you have to walk round a block of stone the size of a cottage—that is but one splinter of the fallen sister that once stood head to head with it.

That is the last individual ruin I remember. By now it was a jungle of stone to me—blue, light, and black shadow, checkered and intertwined in every kind of fantastic impossibility. It was not an impression, it was not an effect: it was sheer bewilderment. Here was a slumbering sphinx, and there the stump where a sphinx had been; there a huge pillar, that had lost itself; there a temple with its stone roof hanging down in rags inside it; a headless body above you tottering against a pictured wall; a bodiless head below you, filling a large pit by itself, gasping up at the vault of heaven ; then a sudden circle of monkey - heads on low pedestals, grinning at each other by the pale moonlight. Finally, the whole destruction seen from the loftiest pylon : a tossing sea of stone—shapes leaping up in struggle, shapes bowed down in despair, shapes tangled, gnarled, and writhed together or apart ; around them the eternal desert, above them the everlasting sky, all dead silent—a prodigy of unutterable collapse.

February 11.—For the last of Luxor we will take something less stupendous, something simpler and therefore more pathetic. Cross the Nile and ride half an hour through the sugar-cane stumps and the clover. There rise up suddenly the twin colossi of Memnon. At their feet tiny Arabs bustle and bellow ; beside them tiny oxen tug at a creaking wheel. They sit with their immense hands resting meekly on their knees, their sightless eyes turned searchingly towards the new risen sun. The ancients fabled that when the first ray of morning struck Memnon he gave out a bell - like clang in answer. But the

joyous sun strikes him and his mate, and
they are silent; it burns on them, and they
are cold; it marches up before their eyes, and
they do not see. Worn and battered, patient,
vast, and so very old, they reproach the all-
seeing sun with their bleared, blind eyes:
they seem to be asking him what has become
of them and theirs that were once so glorious,
of their shivered homes, and their mute, irrecoverable companions.

The Sphinx.

XXI.

THE DAHABEAH.

ASSOUAN—AN ARAB BARD—LIFE ON A DAHABEAH—HOW THE
NATIVES CELEBRATE A "FANTASIA."

February 12.—Assouan is the southern frontier of Egypt, the terminus of the Lower Nile.
And it looks like a terminus. We came to it
on a lazy afternoon, too late for coffee, too
early for tea. The Nile, which had been
lazy too, began to show signs of a current.
We tied up by a bank of yellow sand: in
front of us, to the left, was a long line of
palms with white houses peeping from behind
them — Assouan. Beyond it a lofty rise of
rock—at least, it looks lofty in Egypt—met
the elevation of a rocky, tree-grown island—
Elephantine. Between the two came down
the river, still fretting from the Cataract.

It narrowed between the two elbows of rock, and turned a corner, so that it looked as if Assouan were not only the end of Egypt, but the end of the Nile.

In a quarter of an hour I was in a boat, amid my packages, pulling away up-stream for my friend's dahabeah. Lucky are the friends of my friend, for there is no corner of the world where you may not meet him, and his welcome always gives you to believe he came to this particular corner expressly to meet you. Now I was to live a couple of nights aboard his dahabeah. I had seen the sort of comfort in which Mr Cook will send you up the Nile in a party; now for the luxury when he gives you a dahabeah to yourself.

The six leather-skin rowers took hold of their clumsy oars, one hand like a cap over the butt, swung them out by the loop-of-rope rowlocks, and bent forward. As the oars took the water a seventh leather-skin, squatting idle in the bows, suddenly set up a nasal wail. I knew it at once—Arab singing; but to my horror the whole crew joined in full-throated. For half-a-dozen strokes they howled, and then set up one strident staccato "a-a-ah!" which is the cry they use in this country to remind shirking camels and donkeys of their duty. Then for another six strokes they howled; then a-a-ah-d again to keep themselves up to their work. All the time the idler in the bows kept whining and grunting with a kind of modest enthusiasm. Well he might, for he was the musician of the crew. The Arab sailor won't take the river without a bard to soothe and stimulate him as he rows. He can't do without him. I could.

So we slowly furrowed up the water, dancing golden in the sloping sun, till we came under the leftward shore of Elephantine. And there—where was I? At Henley or in Oxford for the Eights? For there lay moored a row of half-a-dozen white-painted houseboats —houseboats, if you please, at the far-end of Egypt, eight hundred miles from the sea. But on examination they were not exactly like houseboats either. The after-part was

like it, with many windows and awning,
cushions, and lounge chairs; forward the
boats were low in the water and sharp-nosed,
as if built for sailing. They carried a mast
and the yard of an enormous lateen sail that
looked as if it were balanced on top of the
mast, and sloped upwards from just above the
bow till it hung towering almost over the
uprising stern.

That was a dahabeah—or, rather, just half
of one. For this was a sort of yacht with
auxiliary steam in the shape of a tug to
tow it up stream when winds are light and
current contrary. With the lateen sail and
the tug together you can't go wrong — but
for the moment, what had I to do with the
tug? For the boat had come alongside,
fouling the proprietor's fishing-line in its
merry Arab way; in a minute we were
aboard and in the saloon. Many people
would be only too glad to have that saloon,
lying placidly six hundred miles from the
nearest possible upholsterer and decorator, for
their drawing-room at home. Fine furniture,

books, pictures, piano—and these the setting
for that crowning blessing of civilisation, an
English lady. Then dinner, with everything
that the Nile can furnish, or that can be
persuaded by any device of science to keep
during the journey, good wine, good service,
good bed—and not a minute's trouble to the
people who enjoy it. They just order a
dahabeah — and the dahabeah is there,
equipped down to the last table-napkin.
That means a complete holiday—a real holiday. Just as you get a ready-made hotel in
the Nile steamer, so in the dahabeah you get
a ready-made home.

February 13.—The sun of Assouan has only
been up half an hour by seven at this time
of year, but already it is hot on your cheek.
It is a stimulating sun, though, as yet, and
not a deadening one; it wants only half an
hour to stir all Egypt into laughing life.
But when I went out at seven the crew of
the dahabeah were limp and listless. I asked
one of them how he was feeling. The grin is
always on the lips of the Egyptian, and it

broke out right enough, only with it came a groan. "Fantasia," he moaned, and tapped his forehead—"fantasia."

I don't wonder: for last night was a fantasia indeed. It is the custom of the dahabeah hands—dating, presumably, from the days when a voyage up the Nile was a thing of difficulty and danger—to ask their patron on arrival at Assouan for a sheep wherewith to make merry. Some give it and some do not; but if I could only hope to write down the result of that sheep one-tenth as funny as it was, you would agree that a whole sheep-run has often brought in less enjoyment. There was also hasheesh and brandy — they called it brandy — and, perhaps, they too are not without their share of credit for the entertainment.

We were peacefully dining when the first discordant yell surged in through the glass doors. The fantasia has begun, we merely said; and not till we went out to sit on the upper deck did we realise what a fantasia of fantasias was this. As we came

aboard I had noticed that the ship was all
trimmed with lanterns; now they were all
blazing. White and green, red and blue,
they traced out the lines of the upper
deck, the stanchions of the awning, and
climbed to the masthead. By their half
light you could divine that the boat was
also wreathed with feathery sugar-canes.
On a little flat rock a boat's length or two
out in the stream blazed a joyous tar-barrel.
But that was all nothing. With one simul-
taneous wild shriek we all seized on the
nearest support and tried to hold ourselves
upright while we laughed at the crew.

They were all crowded into the low fore-
part of the dahabeah, but at first we could
hardly see them for the noise. There must
have been at least one hundred of them
packed in there, and from every nose issued
skirling indescribable. It kept time, and
kept a kind of tune — kept it only too
faithfully, for it repeated itself every other
bar. They were not all singing, for it seems
that not all Arabs can make the noise to

their own satisfaction; a double row of grave, black - hooded figures at either bulwark merely surveyed the scene with solemn enthusiasm.

But all the rest gave forth grunts, and groans, and wails, and screeches fit to wake the dead and kill the living. It had time, as I say, and a kind of tune, and its quality of sound is best described as the voice of a camel crossed on a bagpipe. That was the outer ring; inside was a double row of musicians and the dancers. There were only two instruments at first—the water-jar, which is slung on the performer and slapped on the bottom like a tom-tom; and a pair of tiny, tiny wooden drums, one the shape and size of a breakfast-cup, the other of a tea - cup. An old man played them: he was not smiling like the others, but very grave; he did not even look at the dancers, — he just tap - tapped away at his baby drums. Nobody could possibly hear their little patter in that ear - achy jangle; but what was that to him? He just tapped on. The breakfast-cup rolled over exhausted; he carefully helped it up, and tapped it some more. A dancer galumphing down the line kicked over the tea-cup; he crawled after it, methodically put it in place, and tapped it again.

Fiercest Bacchanals of all were the dancers. From two to six swayed up and down the line intermittently—now moving slowly, now prancing with emphasis, now banging their feet down on deck in a fury of enjoyment. One especially I had noticed as a singularly languid and incompetent oar in the day; how different now! Now his turban, with a bit of sugar-cane stuck through it, was down over his left eye; from the left corner of his mouth there shot up to meet it a dead cigarette-stump in a holder. His eyes now lit with delight, now quenched with drunkenness. Every limb and every gesture spelt a mixture of insane fury and imbecile good-fellowship. Now he seized a water-bottle and slung it on, tom-tommed up and down, reeled as he kicked his legs abroad and brought them down slap, slap on the deck. Now he was a mixture between a mad bull and a marionette. Then suddenly there appeared in the ring — whence and how he got there nobody knew or cared—a white - haired, jet - black old man, a feather dust - brush stuck through his turban, playing a lyre. Of course you couldn't hear it, but plainly he was playing. A shriek of ecstasy greeted him. He moved his stiff limbs in a desperate dithyramb, and beamed all over with dirt and delirium.

There were one hundred and twenty guests, and they consumed between them only four bottles of brandy and eighteen pennyworth of hasheesh. Yet it was universally agreed to be the fantasia of the season. The noise ceased before midnight, but hours after we went to bed we could hear a crunch, crunch overhead as they chewed at sugar - cane. The crew were eating the decorations.

XXII.

THE ANCIENT EGYPTIANS.

ANCIENT EGYPTIAN ART—RAMESES THE GREAT—CHARACTER OF
THE PEOPLE—A NATION OF MONUMENTAL MASONS.

February 14.—If a modern child were to draw on its slate the masterpieces of ancient Egyptian art, it would be smacked. The form of the buildings, its careful parent would point out, is uncouth and clumsy, and the figures quite hopelessly out of drawing. The men look like wooden dolls, and the women like those india-rubber things that you punch because they have a whistle at the back.

When you point out these fairly obvious facts to the Nile pilgrim, he — it is more usually she—at first catches her breath. Ancient Egyptian art not beautiful! Oh, Mr Steevens!

But when you gently lead her up to Rameses or Cleopatra, and compel her to look at them as she would look at any other carving on any other wall, then she is compelled to allow that the thing is a grotesque abortion. "Oh, but you forget," she says then, "how very old it is: you can't expect much from that age."

When you urge that plea you give Egyptian art away at once : you are beginning to excuse it as the work, not of people whose civilisation might set us blushing for our own, but as primitive barbarians who knew no better. But the queer thing is that a great many of the most admired masterpieces are not so very old after all. The temples of Denderah, Esneh, and Edfu were none of them completed much before the Christian era ; some considerably later. That means that they are more than four hundred years younger than the Parthenon—which was itself the youngest of the great Greek temples. And the rude caricature of Cleopatra on the back of Denderah was scratched there many generations after the Venus of Milo. Not only, it follows, had the ancient Egyptians no art in themselves, but they were incapable of learning better from those who had.

The truth is that the ancient Egyptians were, and remained, barbarians. The civilised idea of producing fine art is to make it beautiful: the barbarous idea is to make it large. Civilised art seeks unity; barbarous art reduplication. Rameses the Great thought he was sure to make himself impressive if he only put up his statues large enough and enough of them in one row: he only succeeded in making himself ridiculous. In a single temple he had forty colossi of himself, and he added figures of his queen standing about as high as his knee; with the result that even worshipping Chicago forgets itself for a moment to laugh at him. He thought we should respect him if he pictured himself thrashing hundreds of similar captives with two similar cats-o'-nine-tails brandished by two similar right arms: we only feel he was no sportsman. Poor Rameses the Great!

So with their architecture. A civilised nation, such as the Greeks were in matters of art, makes a series of pillars all alike : the aim is one single effect. The barbarous Egyptians—though they were actually ruled by Greek kings at the time — made every capital different, and destroyed the unity of effect at once : you cannot see the temple for looking at the capitals. To put it very plainly, the lion - head railing outside the British Museum, which the authorities smilingly spudded up to give the babies and babus of Bloomsbury more pavement, was more beautiful than all the monuments of ancient Egypt put together.

Then, why pay a pound and sixpence farthing to visit them, you cry? But not so fast. The pictures in the Royal Academy are not beautiful ; yet you rightly pay money to see them. Just so the monuments of Egypt are worth seeing ; they are so large, so elaborate, so informative, so old. The ancient Egyptians were not a glad or humorous people. They took everything very

seriously, including themselves. That is their
great secret : they took themselves very, very
seriously. Nine times in ten this made them
ridiculous ; the tenth, it made them sublime.

Was a temple to be built? It should be
the hugest on record, and no expense nor
labour (other people's labour, of course) was
more than the occasion was worth. The
temple may be hideous when you see it ;
there remains the prodigy, that it should
exist at all. It is not the lines of the
building and the carvings that are worth
coming hundreds of miles to see : it is the
tantalising wonder how the devil they got
there. I saw in the old quarries at Assouan
yesterday an obelisk half cut out, but in-
complete, and never carried away. The
sand has blown up over it, and only a little
bit of one surface is left uncovered, but
what remains is big enough to make a
cricket pitch on. The astounding thing
about these gigantic works is that nobody
has ever found the tools with which they
were made ; therefore people believe the

stone was split by driving in wet wooden wedges, and letting them swell. Certainly there are smooth rock faces in the quarries with square marks very like a row of wedges. But whatever it was done with, it is very clear that men with ambition to plan, with energy and patience to carry through, works of such weight and difficulty, were no common barbarians after all.

And then there is the age of it—for when it is really old, how immemorially old it is! Until you come to Egypt you have gone about calling chits of things like Westminster Abbey and the Elgin Marbles and Stonehenge old. In Egypt you begin to understand what o-l-d spells. We talk of ancient Greece, but Egypt had got through twenty dynasties — not twenty kings, but twenty dynasties — before ancient Greece began at all. It had nearly finished its independent history before Romulus was born. Ancient Egypt was all over and done with centuries before Westminster

Abbey was dreamed of. There were old cities in the Euphrates valley—perhaps older than Egypt; that is more than seven thousand years old, at least — but they have left no record of themselves. To-day the monuments of Egypt are the only really ancient remains in the world.

And what manner of people were they, these great-uncles of humanity? It is not their fault if we do not know all about them. Above all things they strove for immortality, and if the bridging of fifty to seventy centuries is near enough for them, they ought to chuckle in their mummy-cases at their success. They have bequeathed to us not only their own bodies, but also their whole daily life, scraped on stone. And though artistically they are barbarians, mechanically they had attained an astoundingly high industrial skill. In the realm of mechanical civilisation they probably knew everything the world knew up to a hundred years ago, except printing, gunpowder, and

the compass. On the top of this they probably had many small devices which the
world now would gladly recover and cannot.

In the earliest days, if I may judge from
their own monuments, the Egyptians were
of a rich umber colour, well made in chest
and arms, but falling away below the waist;
their costume was a simple white petticoat
to the knee. Their wives were yellow ochre
in colour, and wore nothing at all. Their
faces give the impression of having been
flattened with butter patters applied on the
scalp and under the chin. Their expression
is mild and contemplative : in that of
Rameses the Great there is a trace of pawki-
ness; he must have been a chubby little
fellow, and looks rather like a good-tempered
baby in a false beard.

As for their life, it was like enough to
that of Egypt to-day. They were much on
the Nile, fishing, in boats hardly different
from the native dahabeah; they irrigated;
they grew grain, and all kinds of vegetables.

In war they were a scourge to their neighbours—at least, they say they were; naturally, they put up no monument when their
neighbours scourged them. They appear to
have held their wives in small estimation,
and their slaves in none.

But why pretend to talk of the life of the
ancient Egyptians? They took no interest
in life at all, but set their constant minds
only on death. They considered their houses
as lodgings, says Herodotus finely, and their
tombs as their real homes. If anybody ever
lived to die, they did. Only two things
were important to them — the welfare of
their souls, and the solidity of their monuments. They never seem to have built anything but temples to the one end, and tombs
to the other. Their popular literature was
a work called the 'Book of the Dead.' They
were so busy preparing to die that they can
hardly have had any time to live. When-
ever they met and talked together—if they
ever did — I am sure they never laughed,

but spoke in low voices about the splendid
time they meant to have when they were
buried.   Ancient Egypt was one great pre-
paratory school for the cemetery—a nation
of monumental masons.

XXIII.

THROUGH NUBIA.

THE FIRST CATARACT—PHILÆ—NUBIA—THE NATIVE TELEGRAPH
—SUNRISE FROM KOROSKO—ABU SIMBEL—WADY HALFA.

February 15.—A dusty, ramshackle, seven-mile railway took us round the cataract from Assouan to Shellal. There lay Cook's steamer, Prince Abbas, which plies between the first and second cataracts. Our bank of the river was streets of piled-up boxes of bully beef and sacks of flour; up and down them, brick-red monocle in his eye, his legs in khaki trousers, so stout and dusty that they looked like corduroy, walked the same little subaltern whose cabin I shared when first I came out in December. The round peg had dropped straight into the round hole; he walked and watched and gave his orders, energetic, ready, and resourceful, with no theory, but any amount of practice—a pocket edition of the British Empire.

On the opposite bank, as if to reproach the strenuous Empire of to-day, rose up the ghost of the Empire of the past. The tall brown

Island of Philæ in the Nile, above Assouin.

gateway of Philæ temple upreared itself massively in face of us; among rocks and trees to right and left of it peeped out the shamefaced relics of walls and colonnades. The pilgrims from the Rameses the Great were being

ferried across to inspect the ruins. Sorrow-
fully I had waved my hat at each several one
of them—except Jack, who with the ingrati-
tude of his age and sex had already forgotten
his intimate friend, and was busy failing to
make a cat's cradle. Now they struggled up
a little hill and began to spread out over the
island. I thought I heard the distant boom
of Mohammed's "dees way-y-y." I realised
how ridiculous we must have looked when we
went ashore together—and also how very
much we had enjoyed ourselves.

Now we were swinging slowly round in
the narrow, shallow stream; now we were
steaming full up river through Nubia. Nubia
is not in Egypt, and it does not look like it.
You have come into quite a new country—
golden sand instead of rich, brown soil, purple
rock in place of green. Just above the cataract the belt of cultivation—which in Egypt
was often miles and miles of young crops—
vanishes utterly. Harsh rocks run down to
the water's edge; where they recede it is only
to give way to unharvested sand.

Later, when the banks flatten again, there is a little cultivation, but very little. Now and again you pass a row of water - hoists following regularly one on another. These, by the way, are the native telegraph of Egypt. News is shouted by the men at one to the men at the next, and so astoundingly fast does it fly that the death of the last Khedive was known thus at Assouan as soon as by the wire. But the line of them is a very broken one through Nubia; and even where you see them the crops of broad beans and lentil-lupins are the narrowest ribbon along the shore—hardly broader than a railway allotment at home. The country has its uncanny beauty; the brilliancy of the orange sand takes all the blue out of the sky, and leaves a wonderful, soft, colourless belt along the horizon; but its beauty is the beauty of the desert. It is a poor land. Villages are scarce and lightly peopled; almost the whole population of Nubia goes forth to seek its bread in house and stable service wherein Nubians excel all Egyptians for honest faithfulness. Sometimes you land at a little temple: it stands by itself in the drifting sand; no village near, and hardly a wandering soul to ask for backsheesh. The very Nile himself, the life-giver, has changed his character. Here is the wonderful sight of a great river flowing through a parching desert. Between his hard, dry banks he travels purposely, glancing neither right nor left. Somehow the river looks preoccupied. He is not a native here—he is a passenger. His business lies in Egypt, and Nubia he pushes straight through unheeded.

February 16.—"Ding dong, ding dong, at seven o'clock to-morrow," our Mohammed used to remark, when duty bade him announce an especially irritating early start. On this upper reach it appears to be ding dong at five every morning. This morning it was the ascent of the holy Mountain of Korosko in order to see the sun rise. Why should anybody want to do so wild a thing? Everybody who has been obliged to see sunrises knows that as a rule they are the poor-

R

est possible performance, and that clouds
almost invariably rise instead of the sun.
However, the enthusiasts were called at five,
and made so much noise about it that I got
up at six myself, and made a record-breaking
ascent of the heap of shale they call a mountain. At the top you find the stones, whether
fixed or lying loose about the place, all
scratched over with Arabic—the names of
pilgrims who have come to the shrine of the
Korosko saint.

The sun then rose.

There was a good deal of disappointment
at this, as it had been widely anticipated that
it would somehow rise differently here than
anywhere else. There still remained, however, as per guide-book, the view of the desert
route to Khartoum. Over this the young
ladies pretended to be enthusiastic, but here
also it was easy to see that they had expected
something more. Though what it was I cannot guess, for you get a six-mile view of the
caravan track as it winds in and out the bases
of the rough hills. This is about the nearest

route from the Nile across its bend to Abu
Hamed; it is the old camel path, and ought
in theory to have been the starting-point of
the new Sudan Military Railway. But the
rocks made that impossible within the given
limits of time and money. So that the desert
line runs from Wady Halfa to Abu Hamed;
and some day, when the time comes for direct
railway communication between Cairo and
Khartoum, the line may be built from Assouan — not to Halfa, but across the desert
to join the S.M.R. as it nears Abu Hamed.
Cairo-Assouan-Abu Hamed-Berber-Metemneh-
Khartoum, or else Cairo - Assouan - Halfa-
Dongola-Metemneh-Khartoum; the question
appears to lie between these two routes, for
the Sudan will hardly carry them both. The
first has the advantage that the sections
Cairo-Assouan and Abu Hamed-Berber will
be completed this year, while the rails and
sleepers of the Halfa-Abu Hamed line could
be torn up, and the road laid backwards from
Abu Hamed to Assouan.

By now the sun has got up to some purpose, and you can see the Nubian Desert and Nubia. The web of shining gold and purple sand and rocks, stretches limitlessly both sides of the river. And just below you is the little plot of Nubia—the grey-brown mud huts of Korosko, hundreds of them huddled into one small village. Beside them the grateful vividness of just a field or two of green corn. The Nile is nothing but a sun-scaled serpent winding over the desert; from this height he is more than ever a passing traveller, hardly concerning himself with Nubia's forlorn little patch of green. He is journeying to his Egypt. You never heard him called the river of Nubia, nor yet, for all the thousands of miles he goes, anything else than the river of Egypt.

February 17.—From the condemnation of old Egyptian art I passed the other day I must now except Abu Simbel. It is the most original and by far the most impressive of the ancient monuments. We saw it first at night by flaring limelight. The temple is hewn out of a solid cliff of red sandstone. The door is

a low one; the squared face and the interior
very high.   Here again, as in all the other
temples, the mechanical wonder of the achieve-
ment is more than the beauty of it.   Yet Abu
Simbel, if not beautiful, is grand.   For, two
on either side of the doorway, sit four colossal
statues, carved in relief out of the rock face.
They are so well proportioned that they do
not strike you as immense, but how immense
they are you may judge from the fragments
of one that has fallen.   In the morning there
they sat—one defaced, three almost perfect,
leaning in quiet majesty against the precipice,
gazing across the river to the climbing sun.
The interior of the temple is nothing, and
there are no houses nor any buildings near,
nor any growth or other sign of life.   Nothing
at all in sight but those four great, silent
serene warders by the door, looking change-
lessly out over the river to the desolation.

Thence, in the early afternoon, we came to
wind - swept Wady Halfa — the end of our
journey—for so many years the end of the
authority of Egypt.   Few towns have had

more varying fortunes in the last two decades.
It was always bound to exist, because it is at
the foot of the second cataract. Once it was
to be the great terminus of Ismail's railway to
Khartoum. In Egypt's evil days it was a

Wady Halfa from the Nile.

great fortress and garrison town—which is
why its little bazaar of Tenfikish is warned off
to a mile below it. Five years ago raiding
dervishes crept round the town, and hacked
and stabbed through all the bazaar. To-day

Halfa is almost bare of garrison, but all day it clanks, and crashes, and rings with the labour of transport and railway engineering. It looks no longer backward to Egypt, which it used to guard, but forward to the conquests for which it purveys. Which is one more token, for the very end of your journey, that England is going through with her work in Egypt.

Street in Wady Halfa.

XXIV.

COOK.

February 18.—To the general English mind
Cook represents a sort of machine which sits
in Ludgate Circus and punches little holes in
tickets. It never occurred to me, somehow,
that Cook might be a man. But he is. I
have seen him, and spoken with him, and
eaten with him, and voyaged with him four
days, and he is very much a man indeed.

Is it not a wonderful chance to meet with
Cook in the flesh? It would hardly be more
stirring to meet the Attraction of Gravitation
in a Terai hat standing solidly at Assouan

Railway Station. People like Cook, Carter Paterson, or Barclay Perkins, we just accept as part of the necessary organisation of the world : to me, at any rate, it never occurred that they were real people. Nor am I the only person to whom Cook was a sort of law of nature, but who was undeceived. Some years ago Mr J. M. Cook was dining in a hotel opposite two ladies from Boston, who assured him of their own personal knowledge that there was no longer any member of the firm called Cook, but that the business had come entirely into American hands. " I was very interested to hear it," says Mr Cook, with that genial grimness which is all his own ; " but before I'd done I managed to convince 'em that I was myself."

That is just what he does do : he manages to convince everybody that he is himself. He has been doing it in Egypt especially for some thirty years up and down the Nile ; and in Egypt, consequently, they know that Mr Cook is himself perhaps better than we do generally at home. One of the first persons to realise the interesting fact was the dragoman of the very first tourist steamer which young Mr Cook—he was then "and Son"—took up the Nile. For since he was insubordinate and impertinent, Mr Cook threw him into the Nile at Luxor to think it over there, and dragomanned his party up to Assouan himself.

A man like this was just the man for Egypt. He knew what he wanted, and he meant to get it: he did get it, and, what was as much to the point, it was the right thing to want. Up and down the Nile he went; he knew all the dragomans and the boat-captains—and they came to know him. For a small thing, just to show you, the early steamers were steered by a tiller: as the pilot had to sit right forward, so as to see the channel, the tiller became unearthly long and infernally clumsy. But the pilots wouldn't hear of steering by a wheel—it had never been done on the Nile, they pointed out, and therefore it never could be done. So Mr Cook built his boat with a wheel, and steered her himself. Now the steamer pilots look down on their unfortunate brethren who have no wheel, and wonder how they can possibly do with that clumsy tiller.

At first he ran the Egyptian Government's steamers; then he built the Prince Abbas. A high-built, flat-bottomed boat like that, though, said the wise men of Egypt, would capsize in the first gale. And when she lay for days in his arsenal at Bulac, without going out for her trials, they opined that the madman Cook was punished for his rashness at last. "But I was waiting for a gale of wind," explains Mr Cook, and when the barometer promised one he went down to the arsenal and ordered everything ready for the trial. "Better wait," said the manager; "there's a gale coming." "That's just why I'm taking her out," said Mr Cook; and out he took her, and she was steady as a rock. No more whispering about the stability of Cook's Nile steamers after that.

And what does he look like? He looks as you would expect him to look. Tall and strongly knit, he stands erect and firm on his legs to-day, though his beard is snow-white and his round forehead is bare. His white eyebrows bristle resolutely over just the eyes that such a man ought to have—eyes that look out of their sockets like a gun out of a port, blue eyes that seem to have a backward surface looking at the brain, eyes that think as well as see. They must be as clear and his voice as full and firm to-day as when he ducked the dragoman; his movements and gait, I am afraid, are a little stiffer, but they are strong, and it is the gait of a man who knows whither he is going and intends getting there. Altogether a man of force—a man also of humour, of much kindness, but primarily a man of force. I would sooner have him for my friend than for my enemy. Yet I would sooner have him for my enemy than most men; for he would hit straight, and expect to be hit straight back.

Apply this kind of man to a country like Egypt and you will get results. The results in Mr Cook's case are, first, his own success, the establishment of the largest British business in Egypt; second, the opening up of Egypt as a holiday - land to all the world; third, a vast benefit to Egypt herself. Of the private prosperity of Thomas Cook & Son (Egypt), Limited, it is not in my power, and it is not my business, to tell you; but I can give, and have given, you a few hints about the wonderful organisation which deserves and commands success. Perhaps you think I have said too much. But you wouldn't if you were in Egypt, for in a land of wonders I do not know but that the ramifications of Cook & Son are the most wonderful feature. In Egypt he who puts himself into the hands of Cook can go anywhere and do anything. Whether it be the transport of an army or the regulations for the use of a steamer's bath-room, you will find every point thought of, and every point thought out.

That, of course, is why Egypt is full of strangers. They are beginning to leave Cairo by now, I expect, though there are still a few weeks of Egyptian season left. Anyhow, we are near enough to the end to know that this has been the fullest and the most brilliant season that Egypt has ever had. Some people say there have been 50,000 visitors, though that seems impossible; yet the hotels of Cairo will hold, I suppose, nearly 2000 visitors, and they change continually. Of the gaieties of the season I can tell you little; I was not there to enjoy myself. But every night there was a dance somewhere or other, and there were races on the palm - fringed course at Gezireh; I did so far forget myself as to attend these, and the wind cut for all the world like our native Newmarket's.

One thing is certain, and that is that Cook's facilities have resulted in a prodigious influx of every nation into Egypt for the winter time. They come from every country you would know, and from every other one besides: I have met Swedes, Portuguese, Siamese, and Brazilians in the course of the same day. British and American predominate, but perhaps what strikes you most is the swarm of Germans. Ten years ago you would have said

they had neither the money nor the enterprise
to take them farther than Naples. To-day
you meet them everywhere. We had a sing-
song on one of the tourist steamers coming up,
and a German, being asked to play by some
practical joker, gave us forty-five minutes of
the "Nibelung's Ring." There was nothing,
given your German, extraordinary in that:
the striking point was that there were enough
Germans round to give him a hand. The German in Egypt gets himself up exactly in the
manner of the comic Englishman of the Continental circus. Men in huge helmets, with
huge puggary, huge blue goggles, knicker-
bockers, and chess-board stockings; women in
the same helmets and goggles, vast blue veils,
sunshade, short skirts, and vast hands and
feet; both sexes crested with Meyer or
Baedeker rampant—they make a picture at
which native Egypt gapes in undisguised
delight.

Lastly, Mr Cook is a blessing to Egypt—
perhaps the only one of Egypt's recent bless-

ings which nobody disputes. It is not only the vast amount of money he brings into the country, nor the vast number of people he directly employs. Besides that, you will find natives all up the Nile who practically live on him. Those donkeys are subsidised by Cook; that little plot of lettuce is being grown for Cook, and so are the fowls; those boats tied up on the bank were built by the sheikh of the Cataracts for the tourist service with money advanced by Cook.

Therefore, when "the Governor" is pleased to travel up and down his Nile, you may see the natives coming up to him in long lines, salaaming and kissing his hand. When he appears they assemble and chant a song with refrain, "Goood-mees-ta-Cook." Once he took Lord Cromer up the Nile, and they went to visit a desert sheikh somewhere at the back of Luxor. The old man had no idea that the British had been possessing Egypt all these years — barely knew that the late Khedive was dead.

"Haven't you ever heard of me?" asked

Lord Cromer.   No; the sheikh had never heard of Lord Cromer.

"Have you heard of Mr Cook?"

"Oh, yes; Cook Pasha—everybody knows Cook Pasha."

XXV.

LOOKING BACK AND FORWARD.

THE APPROACH OF SUMMER — THE ESSENTIAL EGYPT — BACK-
SHEESH — ENGLISH WORKERS IN EGYPT — THE PICK OF THE
WORLD — THE DANGER OF AN UNCONQUERED SUDAN — INTER-
NATIONAL BURDENS — NO CHANCE OF OUR LEAVING EGYPT.

February 21.—Now we have come to the
very end of Egypt, and stepped over the
threshold of the Sudan, it is natural to look
back for a moment down the Nile. Day by
day it is dropping down its banks, and each
mail steamer comes up a little more delayed,
by running ashore, than the last. Each
morning a little more black mud is laid
bare at the water's edge. In mid - stream
three days ago there appeared a shadow;
yesterday it had darkened to a black bank;
to - day there are natives wading over it,

staking out their melon - patches. Summer is close on us—the torrid Sudan summer, which begins in March. The water is changing from brown to green, which means that the Abyssinian mud is all exhausted, and what passes us now is the rainfall and decayed green-stuff of Uganda. This is the back of the wonderful page of Egypt's fertility —the opening of the months of sterility and dust and parching heat.

When you come to Egypt be sure you come up the Nile, for until then you have not begun to see the essential Egypt. The mud huts and the water-wheels, the clumsy ploughs and unhandy mattocks, the buffaloes and donkeys, the palms and green corn—it is all very Egypt, now and seven thousand years ago. And it all has a flavour that is like nothing else in the world. Egypt is neither Europe, Asia, nor Africa : set at the corner of all three, it takes character from each, and overlays it with a filmy something of its own. It is European politically, Asiatic industrially, African geographically ; yet its

politics are all its own, its industries are not
quite like any other, and the lands it seems
to bound are, in fact, the farthest away
from it.   (

How so? Because of the Nile. The river
makes the best part of its external politics;
the existence of a living river near this desert
gate between east and west gives it all its
external importance. The river shapes its
arts and handicrafts, and turns them into
variations which find a place nowhere else
in the world. The river, finally, by a miracle
of geography, husbands itself through two
thousand miles of desert, to pour all its
riches into the lap of Egypt. There is no
other country in the least like Egypt, because
there is only one Nile.

Then again, unless you go up the Nile
you will hardly see the Egyptian. You will
answer that you do not want to see the
debased and parasitic Egyptian who cringes
for backsheesh. But that, I am afraid, is
just the Egyptian you ought to see; add
hard work, and that is just the Egyptian.

He is industrious—in winter; in summer he does nothing — there is nothing to do; enduring and cheerful; but there his virtues end. He has no self-control, no honesty, no courage, no independence, no initiative. And unless you keep the curb on him, his industry will vanish, and his cheerfulness turn to impertinence. He was born to ask for backsheesh and do what he is told.

And after all the æons of his wonderful history — after his early strivings towards civilisation, his victories, and his massive, funereal greatness; after his conquest by Persians, Macedonians, and Romans; after his Christianity, his Mussulmanism, and conversion from Copt to Arab, the wars of Crusader and Turk and Mameluke, Frenchman and Englishman — at the end of his sixty-ninth century, he seems at last to have found a master who is telling him to do the right things. The tangle of immemorial confusion and wrong looks like to be unravelled and wound up straight at last.

Of the men who are doing this work for

Egypt, for Britain and the world, whether
in the Government offices or by the Canal
banks, or in camp with their faces towards
Khartoum, we may all be endlessly proud.
Gifted with all the Briton's misfortunes of
manner, and in no way troubling themselves
to cloak their plenitude of authority, they
are disliked in Egypt; but they are obeyed
and they are trusted. No money will buy
the Briton, and no risk will deter him, when
it is a case of duty—that the Arab knows
well. For himself he rather despises that
frame of mind, but as a rule he recognises
its utility. The Briton does his duty, and,
what is more, he does it well. In our country
we are most of us honest and reasonably
ready to take risks if need be; but we are
not all good at our work. The men in
Egypt are: they are all picked men — the
pick of Britain, which is to say the pick of
the world.

What they have done I have tried to sketch
for you; now a word about what is still to do.
And first for the shadow that has hung over

Egypt all the years that England has been there — the Sudan. I cannot see that the Sudan will add a piastre to Egypt's wealth, nor, except as a recruiting-ground, an ounce to her power; yet reconquered the Sudan must be. Run over what we have seen of Egypt, and then try to imagine Egypt without the Nile, or with less Nile. The first means starvation for the whole country, the second distress and the stoppage of all progress. The danger that the Upper Nile might be tapped for irrigation is not, perhaps, a very immediate one, but neither is it altogether imaginary. As long as it is so much as a possibility Egypt must guard against it at all costs, for to her the Nile — and the whole Nile—means daily bread.

You should add to this that the presence of a constantly hostile power on her frontier must be, in time, far more wearing, far more costly, than any campaign. The constant menace keeps the border fortresses awake and the watching armies always on a war footing. Moreover—why not tell the truth?—there is a vast deal of opinion in Egypt, which would be only too delighted to hear of a dervish victory. You won't find that opinion up in Dongola, or even here in Halfa, where the people have tried what a raid feels like, and if the dervishes were to invade Egypt you wouldn't find it anywhere else very long; but at present it exists, and it unsettles things. Egypt will never quite sit down beneath our rule as long as we have an enemy unbeaten in the south; and the very being of Mahdism forbids the possibility that the enemy should ever be a friend. So that the sooner it's over and done with the better for Egypt and everybody.

Until then Egypt can do nothing, because Egypt will be a beggar. When that is done, the weirs at the Barrage and the new barrages at Assouan and Assiut will be her chief work for the next years. We have heard vaguely up here that the contract for these is already signed; though where the money is to come from, the meagre telegrams do not say. Another work of importance is the readjustment of the land-tax, which is arbitrary and inequitable : I do not quite understand why this has not been done before. After that there is still plenty and plenty of work to be done, especially in the way of education. The administration of the railways, again, strikes a stranger as very bad ; while in the domain of justice the Egyptian, much improved, has still to learn enough for very many years.

But the country will not top the Nile difficulty until it can get its international burdens off its back. The inability to tax foreigners adequately, the inability to bring them to trial, the inability to spend her own money—the Capitulations, the Mixed Tribunals, and the Caisse de la Dette—must all go sooner or later. Internally their abolition would at last give Egypt a free hand. She has had a free hand in her history before, and for the last fifteen years she has had a prudent and honest government; but she has never yet had both together. When she gets them we shall see what can be done with her.

Externally, the Capitulations, the Mixed Courts, and the Caisse contribute to a curious deadlock. While they exist Egypt is in tutelage; their existence is sufficient evidence in itself that the civilised world does not consider her fit for independent self-government. Therefore so long as they exist it is vain to ask us to evacuate the country. If Egypt can be trusted, we shall answer, Knock off her fetters. If she cannot, then we stay; for after our past sacrifices we shall assuredly not hand over the work to be worse done by somebody else.

There is no chance of Europe knocking off the fetters, and there is no chance, therefore, of our leaving Egypt. I do not think that we shall ever leave. This is awkward, because we promised to — gave a perfectly sincere promise which we have not been able to fulfil. I do not think we ever shall be able to fulfil it without wasting an enormous deal of splendid work — which we shall not do. Some day, perhaps, we shall square the situation, either by agreement or after a war.

In the meantime, the world is full of Tunises and Chantabuns, 'Kiao - Chaus and Port Arthurs : we need not distress ourselves. The whole world knows, in its heart, that we are staying in Egypt ; and the whole world, in its sleeve, is very well satisfied.

Old mosque tomb.

www.ingramcontent.com/pod-product-compliance
Lightning Source LLC
Chambersburg PA
CBHW020848020726
47497CB00005B/1314